PEANUT BUTTER FRIENDS
in a CHOP SUEY WORLD

Books by Deb Brammer

Peanut Butter Friends in a Chop Suey World

Two Sides to Everything

Moose

PEANUT BUTTER FRIENDS
iñ a CHOP SUEY WORLD

Deb Brammer

journeyforth®

Greenville, South Carolina

Library of Congress Cataloging-in-Publication Data

Brammer, Deb, 1954-
    Peanut butter friends in a chop suey world / Deb Brammer ; illustrations
by Grace Kim.
     p.   cm.
    Summary: Sixth-grader Amy and her family move to Taiwan to do mis-
sionary work, but even at her school for English-speaking students Amy
finds the adjustment difficult.
    ISBN 0-89084-751-7
    [1. Missionaries—Fiction. 2. Taiwan—Fiction. 3. Schools—Fiction. 4.
Christian life—Fiction.   I. Kim, Grace, ill.
    II. Title.
    PZ7.B735788Pe   1994
    [Fic]—dc20   94-38216
                                           CIP
                                            AC

Peanut Butter Friends in a Chop Suey World
Edited by Carin Fagerberg
Cover photo credits: © 2005, Dynamic Graphics, Inc., chopsticks; © 2004,
Brand X Pictures, peanut butter
Illustrations by Grace Kim

© 1994 by BJU Press
Greenville, South Carolina 29614
JourneyForth Books is a divison of BJU Press

Printed in the United States of America
All rights reserved

ISBN 978-0-89084-751-0

15   14   13   12   11   10   9   8   7   6

To my husband, Art,
who brought me to Taiwan
and encouraged me to write;
and to Lori,
who sees and enjoys the beauty in life,
and to Lisa,
who thinks it must be boring
not to be a missionary's kid

Table of Contents

Chapter One
The Big Adventure

The plane's restroom was so tiny I could hardly stand up. The plane was bouncing, which complicated everything, but at least I had a mirror. The biggest adventure of my life was about to begin, and I didn't want to start it until I was neat and tidy.

In just a few minutes we'd be landing in Taiwan. My family and I would actually live in this Chinese country— we'd learn to speak Chinese, and we'd make Chinese friends and win lots of souls for Jesus. If I was going to be a missionary, I wanted to be a good one.

I washed and dried my hands and added the towel to the trash that spilled out of the trash compartment.

The pilot's voice crackled over the intercom. "Ladies and gentlemen, in a few minutes we will be landing in Taipei. Local time is 7:45 P.M."

I checked my watch–4:45 A.M. That was Los Angeles time. Fifteen hours had turned early Tuesday afternoon into Wednesday evening, all because we'd crossed the International Date Line.

I examined myself in the mirror. Fifteen hours ago I had hugged Grandma in a wrinkle-free skirt in Los Angeles. Over the ocean, however, my skirt had creased into wrinkles, turned sideways, and spit out the blouse that had been so neatly tucked in.

"Amy Carmichael Kramer, you look terrible," I told the mirror. The mirror nodded up and down as if it agreed. The bobbing mirror kept time with my stomach and the jolting plane. I'd scare the Chinese away looking like this.

I reached into my pocket for a brush. Cookie crumbs pushed under my fingernails. Fifteen hours had also changed two cookies into a pocketful of crumbs. How could I possibly start my big adventure with a pocket full of cookie crumbs? I tried to pull my pocket up and dump the crumbs into the sink, but succeeded only in smearing chocolate chips across my skirt and jabbing my elbow into the soap dish.

I gave up on the crumbs and found the brush in my other pocket. I tried to brush my hair, but the static electricity just made the long golden strands dance around my head. Amy Kramer, otherwise known to Pinedale, Wyoming's sixth-grade class as "Miss Tidy," was a total disaster.

I jammed the brush back into my pocket and unlocked the door. "Look out, Taiwan. Here I come."

I stumbled around the other people lined up outside the restroom and went on down the lurching aisle. At our row, I fell into the seat at the end. The center section of the plane had five seats in each row. It was just right for my parents, my two brothers, and me.

"Mom, do I look all right?" I asked. Mom was at the other end of the row, sitting by Dad.

"You look fine. The Petersons know we've been in the air a long time. They'll understand."

"Do we really have to call them Uncle Tim and Aunt Martha?" A.J. asked. "They're not even related to us."

"I think you'll want to call them uncle and aunt," said Mom. "Since they're the only other family with our mission board in Taiwan, they'll be just like family to us. And to think they have a girl just a year older than Amy." She looked down the row at me. "Isn't it wonderful how the Lord planned that for you, Amy? Imagine—a best friend right from the start."

If "the start" was now, I hoped Kelly didn't mind making friends with a total disaster.

Dad eyed my little brother Hud, who was patiently coloring a picture of an airplane. "Time to put the crayons and book away, Hud. Then shove your bag under the seat. We're getting ready to land."

Hud put away his book and fastened the seat belt around himself and his stuffed lion. "Are we in Wyoming or California?" To Hud, Wyoming was still home. He knew Grandma lived in California, and he didn't know where Taiwan fit in. Poor kid. Maybe his first-grade teacher could straighten him out.

"We're in Taiwan—all the way across the Pacific Ocean from California," A.J. told Hud. Now that he was in fifth grade, A.J. was getting to know some geography.

Hud hugged his stuffed lion closer. "Amy, do they have peanut butter in Taiwan?"

"Peanut butter is one of the world's basic foods," I said. "Everybody has peanut butter."

"What if they don't?"

"They do. At least I think so."

"Do they have chocolate chip cookies?"

I shrugged. We were getting ready to land—this wasn't a good time to worry about details.

Hud persisted. "What if they don't have chocolate chip cookies?"

"Then we'll just eat another kind of cookie. Like peanut butter cookies."

"What if they don't have peanut butter?"

It *was* hard to imagine living in a country without peanut butter. But I covered my worries with the thought of that great missionary to India, Amy Carmichael. My parents hadn't named me after her for nothing. If she could risk her life to rescue little girls sold as slaves to the temple, I could risk life without peanut butter.

The pilot's voice came over the intercom again. "Ladies and gentlemen, we are about to begin our approach to Chiang Kai Shek International Airport. Please put your seats in their upright and locked position and fasten your seat belts. We'll be landing in a few minutes."

Mom grabbed Dad's arm. "Honey, we're almost there. Can you believe it?"

Dad squeezed her hand. "We've waited a long time for this day."

"Are you sure Mr. and Mrs. Peterson will be waiting for us?" I asked. "And Kelly?"

Dad looked down the row at me. "They know we're coming. Someone will be there."

Our bodies pushed back against the seats as we slowed to landing speed. Then the wheels bumped against the runway.

"We made it!" Dad said.

We got off the plane and waited for our luggage. Then we had to drag all ten suitcases and five carry-ons through customs. The officials glanced through a couple of our suitcases and waved us on. We hauled our suitcases through some doors into a big open area and searched for a friendly face. Finally a giant of a man with a balding head of blond hair rushed around a partition.

"Are you the Kramers?" he asked.

"We sure are," Dad told him.

"Well, welcome to Taiwan!" Mr. Peterson pumped Dad's hand.

"Where's Kelly?" I asked him.

"Kelly and your Aunt Martha had to stay home so there would be room for all your luggage," he said. "I only brought a van, not a ten-ton truck." I looked at our pile of luggage and knew he was right.

"But don't you worry," Uncle Tim said. "We're going to take you to your new home in Taichung. That's a couple of hours away. By the time we get there, a bed is going to look awfully good to you. In the morning you can come to our house for breakfast, and you girls can have a good time getting acquainted."

So I'd have to wait a little longer to meet Kelly, and she'd have to wait to meet me. In my present condition that had its advantages.

I stared out the window of the van, trying to see what Taiwan was like. It was already dark, however, and all I could see was the freeway stretching out before our headlights. Except for the Chinese characters on road signs, we could have been in America.

I stuck my hand into my pocket, and my fingertips searched for the few remaining cookie crumbs. The cookies had flown with me from Jackson Hole to Salt Lake City and then on to Los Angeles. I'd nibbled on them while we were busy visiting with Grandma at the L.A. airport. Now they reminded me of Dawn McGill, my best friend since church nursery days. She had given me the cookies at the airport in Wyoming. "Just in case Taiwan doesn't have chocolate chip cookies," she'd said. She knew how much I loved them.

It hadn't been easy leaving her, but I had tried to think about the new friends I'd make in Taiwan. There'd be Kelly of course. And then my Chinese friends. Would I be able to make friends with the Chinese kids when I couldn't speak Chinese?

I laughed at myself. Dad had always called me his worry wart, and I guess he was right. We hadn't even reached our new home, and I was already worrying about living in Taiwan. The answer was obvious. If I wanted to make Chinese friends, I'd just have to learn Chinese. It would be easy now that we lived here. At least that's what everyone said.

I pictured myself chattering away to my Chinese friends as I sampled an exotic Chinese dish with securely held chopsticks. Then I saw myself surrounded by Chinese people begging me to tell them the gospel. My picture looked like the life of a typical missionary. But it didn't look like me, ordinary Amy Kramer. So far I didn't even know "hello" in Chinese. Would crossing the ocean really make living Chinese-style easy?

I'm in Taiwan now, I thought. That means I already am a foreign missionary. Why don't I feel any different?

Ready or not, my adventure had begun. It would be four more years before we saw America again, and then only for a year of furlough when we would visit the churches that supported us. Taiwan was our home now. America was the foreign country.

Would I like Taiwan? I'd better. Dad could have bought round-trip tickets. But he hadn't. All five of our tickets were one-way.

Chapter Two
Brain Juice and Dragon Eyes

By the time we got to our house in Taichung, I was sound asleep. The next thing I knew, it was morning. A rooster crowed and startled me awake.

The rooster made me think for a moment that I was back on Uncle Pete's ranch in Wyoming. But no, I was in a big Chinese city. Sweat oozed from every pore of my body. Wyoming had never felt like this, even when it was hot. This must be the humidity I had heard people talk about.

I glanced around at the bare walls and windows. This was home? I leaped to the window to see what Taiwan looked like. All I could see was our neighbor's house, about three inches from my window.

Determined to look out, I raced downstairs. Dad had set up a folding chair in the bare living room and was sitting in front of a fan. He was sorting through a suitcase. Hud sat hunched over a book.

Dad must have heard me coming; he put his finger to his lips. "Shhh. Mom's still asleep."

"Dad!" I whispered. "People are looking in our window!"

They were. Three little Chinese kids were hanging on the bars that guarded our window—and they were staring in!

"I noticed," Dad said.

The kids began to chatter away in Chinese. One boy kept saying the same word over and over again. "*A-tok-a.*"

"Why don't you ask them what they want?"

"Because I doubt that they know much English."

"*A-tok-a,*" the boy called out to some other kids walking by. They joined the others at the window. "*A-tok-a,*" they agreed, and they laughed. Soon they got tired of staring and ran off.

"Don't they know it's rude to stare?" I asked.

"Maybe it's not."

"But you always told us. . . ."

"In America it's rude to stare. But we're not in America anymore. Things are going to be different here."

A.J. came flying down the stairs. "Can I go outside?" he yelled.

"Shhh," Dad said. "Go ahead. But try not to wake your mother."

As A.J. opened the door, a small truck drove by. The man driving the truck called out something in Chinese over a loudspeaker.

"Why don't you tell him Mom's sleeping?" A.J. asked. "I think he's selling something. Hey Dad, someone swiped our yard." Dad and Hud went to the door. Since I was still in my pajamas, I just peeked out the window.

"What do you mean?" Dad asked.

"Well, there's no grass. Just concrete. The sides of our house are stuck to the sides of our neighbors' houses. And we don't even have three inches of back yard. I already looked."

Dad offered a lopsided smile. He scratched his head a little. "Well, like I said, 'Things—' "

"—are going to be different here," I finished for him.

I spied a thermometer by the front window. Thirty-five degrees?

"This thermometer's messed up," I said. "It says it's three degrees above freezing."

"That's Celsius," Dad said.

"So how hot is thirty-five degrees Celsius?"

"Almost a hundred degrees, I think. Hot enough, anyway."

While we stared out at the world in front of us, a man who had been buying something from the truck came into our yard. He held out two bags of what he had just bought and said something in Chinese.

"I can't speak Chinese." Dad said every word slowly and clearly. "I'm sorry."

The man held the bags closer to Dad.

"For me?" Dad pointed to himself.

The man nodded.

"Thank you," Dad said. "Thank you very much."

He took the bags and led A.J. and Hud back inside to inspect their contents.

I held up one bag. "It looks like bread dough."

"No, I don't think it's raw," Dad told us. "It's not brown, but it's not raw. It must be steamed or something. This other bag seems to be all liquid." He loosened the tie around the top. He smelled it, taking tiny whiffs at first, gradually inhaling deeply. "Doesn't smell like much. Maybe a little like yeast."

"Oooooh. Looks like brain juice." A.J. took a whiff too. "Even smells like brain juice."

"A.J., that's sick!" I said. "Dad, tell him not to say disgusting things like that."

Dad shrugged. "You never know. A.J. may be right. Maybe it is brain juice."

"Can I taste it?" Hud asked.

"Taste what?" It was Mom. She was up and dressed.

"A Chinese man came and brought us breakfast," Dad told her. "I guess he didn't know we had an invitation."

"I want a taste. I want a taste," Hud said. While we were still discussing the bags, Mr. Peterson—Uncle Tim, that is—pulled up in the van.

"Ready for breakfast?" he asked when Hud let him in.

"We already have some," Hud said. "A Chinese man brought us some."

"A neighbor?"

"Our next-door neighbor." Dad pointed to the side the man lived on.

"In Chinese we call that a 'next-wall neighbor.' That must be Mr. Hwang. He's the one who told us this house was empty and helped us get in touch with the landlord." Uncle Tim picked up the bag of liquid. "Well, what have we here? Looks like *dou-jyang* and *man-tou*."

"A.J. says the juice is brain juice," I said. "Tell him what it really is."

"It's just soybean milk." He handed it to A.J., who began pinching the bag, then letting it swell out again. "The other stuff is steamed bread. A typical Chinese breakfast. You'd like the *man-tou*, the bread. And the soybean milk isn't bad if you're used to it. Kelly likes it."

"And you don't even have anything like brain juice here in Taiwan, isn't that right, Uncle Tim?" I asked him.

"Well, let's see. Pig's brain is supposed to be really good for you. And they have pig's blood soup. But I don't think I've ever heard of brain *juice*."

"You're kidding, right?" I said.

Uncle Tim just shook his head.

A.J. let out a cheer. "All right! I'm going to like this place."

I covered my mouth and headed upstairs to dress. Pig's blood soup? Whatever happened to traditional Chinese food like chop suey and sweet and sour pork?

My mind may have been ready for this big adventure, but my stomach was wishing we'd never left Wyoming.

At the Peterson's house we were greeted by Aunt Martha, Kelly, and the reassuring smell of waffles.

Mrs. Peterson had just a nice amount of plumpness to her and a few streaks of gray in her hair. I thought it wouldn't be too hard to call her Aunt Martha. I could tell that Kelly hadn't dressed up to meet us, but I didn't mind. Her loose T-shirt looked cool and comfortable.

"So how do you like Taiwan?" Kelly asked me. She swept the short brown hair off her forehead with one hand.

"It sure is hot!" And then, so she wouldn't think I was complaining, I added, "But I'm sure we'll like it. We just haven't seen very much of it yet."

I glanced around the Petersons' house. It wasn't fancy, but they had lots of pictures on the walls and pretty drapes at the windows. When we got our crate of things from America, Mom would fix up our house too.

"Well, the waffles aren't getting any warmer," Aunt Martha said when she had met us all. "Come on into the kitchen and find yourself a seat anywhere."

In the kitchen I was glad to see regular white milk in the glasses instead of pale brown soybean milk. Uncle Tim kept the waffle iron busy, so we had plenty to eat. There was homemade syrup or powdered sugar to put on them and (oh joy!) peanut butter. I put peanut butter on my first waffle just to let my stomach know it wouldn't have to get along without it. On the table were bananas and a brown kind of fruit about the size of grapes.

"They're dragon eyes," Kelly told us. "If you pinch them right, they pop out." She showed us how to do it and then held out the cloudy white ball for us to examine.

"Oooooh. It looks like an eyeball," A.J. said.

"Don't pay attention to A.J.," I told Kelly. "He always says stuff like that."

"It's okay." Kelly popped a dragon eye into her mouth. "He's right. They really do look like eyeballs."

A.J. peeled and ate one, too. "Pretty good for eyeballs."

I peeled a dragon eye and sniffed it. It didn't have much smell, so I tasted it. It was okay. Slightly sweet. It felt like a peeled grape in my mouth, only it had a big pit in the middle. I tried to figure out what it tasted like so I could write and tell Dawn about dragon eyes. Finally I gave up. It didn't taste like anything I'd ever eaten before.

After breakfast, Mom and Dad went with Uncle Tim to talk to our new landlord about the house. A.J., Hud, and I stayed at the Petersons'.

"What do you want to do?" Kelly said.

"What do you usually do on summer days?" I asked her. "Pass out tracts?"

She looked at me like I'd come from Mars. "You're kidding, right?" she finally asked.

"Well, n-no. Isn't that what missionaries usually do?"

"My folks are the missionaries. I'm just the kid."

I stared at her. Finally I remembered my manners and looked away. I twirled a lock of hair around my finger.

"Hey, I do my part," she said. "I've always brought my Chinese friends to Sunday school. And I watch the nursery on Sundays. I suppose you spent all your spare time in Wyoming passing out tracts?"

"Well, no. But that was in America. This is the mission field."

"So? This is just another place to live. In the summer I swim, and ride bikes, and read books. Once in a while we go grass-skiing."

"Grass-skiing?" A.J. asked. That probably sounded like his kind of missionary work.

"Sure. We don't have snow here, but we have a few grassy slopes. You can rent grass skis. They're kind of like roller skis with a belt around them. You know, like the wheels on an army tank."

"Sounds like fun," A.J. said.

"I don't even snow ski," I told Kelly. "Looks dangerous to me. I'd rather slide down a hill on an inner tube. Then you don't have very far to fall."

"They have grass toboggans too. Anyone can ride them. The scooters are fun too, though once I broke my sunglasses riding on one."

"It's got to be dangerous to be fun," A.J. said. "I already broke my arm once and my leg twice. I can run faster on crutches than most people can regular."

Kelly smiled. "Hey, A.J., you want to play some badminton?"

"Where?"

"In the street. We'll have to move if a car comes by, but it works okay."

"Can I go first?" he asked.

"We'll do *jong-kong-pai* for it."

"What's that?"

She chanted *"jong-kong-pai,"* shook her fist twice, and then made a *v* with her fingers. "This is 'scissors.' A fist is 'rock.' A flat hand is 'paper.' Paper covers rock—"

"I know," A.J. said. "Scissors cut paper. Rock breaks scissors. Paper covers rock. We do that in America too. The Chinese must get it from America."

"No. It's the other way around," Kelly said. They did their *jong-kong-pai* and went out to play. I watched them go and then picked up a book to read to Hud. As I read, his eyes drooped and I could tell he was sleepy. They'd explained to us about jet lag. Maybe the long trip and changing time zones were catching up with him.

By the time I finished reading *Frog and Toad Together,* Hud was fast asleep and Frog and Toad were still the best of friends. It looked like Kelly and A.J. were too. So who was supposed to be my best friend?

Chapter Three
A Brave New Amy

I wanted to make friends with some of the Chinese neighbor kids, but I didn't know how to begin. Every time I went outside, they stared and pointed and laughed. I wanted them to notice me, but not that much. I wanted them to talk to me too, and yet at the same time I didn't. If they said anything, I wouldn't understand, so how could I answer them?

I spent my first day in Taiwan peeking out of windows, trying to see Taiwan without Taiwan seeing me. I told myself that I was just tired. Later on, I'd make some Chinese friends.

I was still peeking out the window the next day when I thought about Amy Carmichael. She had disguised herself and rescued little girls who were sold to Indian temples. She didn't waste any time peeking out windows. If the first Amy Carmichael was that brave, I could be brave enough to talk to my Chinese neighbors.

Besides, living in Taiwan was my chance to discover what life was like in a foreign country, I told myself. I couldn't get to know the people very well without learning their language. It was time to make a Chinese friend.

Mom and Dad had asked Uncle Tim to take them shopping for furniture. While they went shopping, I planned to stay home and watch Hud and A.J.; at the same time I'd check out the neighborhood from the outside.

The first thing I needed to do was to learn a few Chinese words. I knew I wouldn't be able to say a lot at first, but it was pretty hard to make a friend without saying anything. When Uncle Tim came to get Mom and Dad, Kelly was with him. She was on her way to a friend's house. So I asked Kelly to teach me a few words.

"First I need to know how to say 'hello' and 'good-by,' " I told her.

"Well, let's see." Kelly plopped into one of the five folding chairs that we moved around our house as we needed them. "They don't have a word that just means 'hello.' But you can say *'Ni hau ma?'* That means 'How are you?' "

"Ni hau ma?"

"Right. And then they might say *'Hau.'* That means 'good.' And then they'll ask you back, *'Ni hau?'* And you say, *'Hau.'* "

"Ni hau ma? Hau. Ni hau? Hau." I practiced the sounds to be sure I had them.

"Not too bad," Kelly said. "Just be sure you say it the same way every time. Like when you say *'hau.'* Be sure you start on a medium pitch and then go lower and come up again. Chinese has four different tones, and if you don't use the right tone, you don't get the word right."

I practiced my greeting several more times until Kelly said I had it right. Then she taught me one more word. *"Dzai-jyan,"* she said. "That means 'good-by'."

Mom and Dad were ready to go by the time I finished my language lesson. As they went out the door I called, *"Dzai-jyan*, Kelly. *Dzai-jyan,* Uncle Tim."

"Dzai-jyan."

When they left, Hud was busy coloring, and he hummed a little tune while he worked. He's good at playing by himself.

A.J. was trying to jump from the fifth step to the foot of the stairs. With our concrete floors that wasn't too smart, but I decided I could use a little of A.J.'s bravery right now.

Chinese jabbering filtered in from outside. It was time for me to make my move.

"Ni hau ma? Hau. Ni hau? Hau." I repeated the words over and over again to myself. I glanced out the window. Several girls about my age were playing high jump over a jump rope made of rubber bands.

I put on my shoes and wiped my sweaty hands on my shirt. Maybe I'd better get a drink of water first. I did that and then offered to pour a drink for my brothers. For once they didn't want anything to drink.

"You need anything?" I asked Hud.

"Nope."

"I thought I'd go outside."

Neither of the boys even looked up.

"Ni hau ma?" I whispered as I opened the door.

I walked outside and stood at the gate to our yard. The girls were still playing. They seemed to be arguing about whose turn it was. I tried to say my line but the words wouldn't come out. My mouth felt like it was stuffed full of cotton. Maybe I needed another drink.

After my second drink I was even more determined to talk to the Chinese girls. This time I didn't stop at the gate. I went right out into the road to where they were playing. They stopped playing and stared at me.

"A-tok-a!" they said.

"Ni hau ma?"

They looked at me as if I'd said, "Giraffes have purple teeth," and then burst into giggles.

"Ni hau ma? Ni hau ma? Ni hau ma?" They mimicked me in lightning fast Chinese. *"A-tok-a shuo, 'Ni hau ma?'"* They laughed and hurried away to tell their friends the amazing news.

I stood in the street staring after them. All I said was, "How are you?" What could possibly be funny about "How are you?"

After a few minutes a truck drove up and honked for me to move.

I shuffled back into the house.

"Make some friends?" A.J. asked as I went in.

"Not yet. But that was only my first try."

How could you ever hope to make friends with kids who laughed every time you said, "How are you?"

Oh, well. I would just have to be tough and try again.

On Sunday we got an introduction to church in Chinese. Someday my Dad would start a Chinese church. But while we were learning Chinese, we'd go to a church that Uncle Tim and Aunt Martha had started thirteen years ago. Church was a good place to make friends in America. I figured that

Chinese church would be the natural place to begin making Chinese friends.

Uncle Tim's church met in a building that looked a lot like our house. The church used one house in a strip of about six houses joined together. A Chinese family lived on one side of the church, and on the other side was a little store.

When we got to church, Uncle Tim introduced us to some Chinese workers; he spoke in Chinese. At first Dad reached out to shake their hands; then, trying to be more Chinese, he just nodded. The workers smiled, nodded, and then reached out in awkward handshakes of their own.

A couple of kids in shorts and flip-flops studied me for several minutes, then reached out to touch my hair. I smiled at them. *"Ni hau,"* I said.

They laughed and ran away.

There was only one Sunday school class in the church. That first Sunday I counted fourteen Chinese kids of various ages besides the four of us Americans.

Since A.J. and Hud and I didn't know any of the songs in Chinese, we just sat there feeling stupid. Several of the Chinese kids wiggled out of their seats and wandered around.

"Can I get up too?" Hud whispered to me while the teacher was telling a story in Chinese. Judging from the pictures, it was about David and Goliath.

"No. The teacher's still telling the story."

"But the other kids are doing it, and some of them are older than I am."

"Shhh."

"But I can't understand what the teacher is saying."

"Shhh!"

After forty-five minutes of Sunday school we didn't understand, we sat through an hour of church we didn't understand. By noon, for the first time in my life, I couldn't wait to get out of church. I'd never thought missionary life would be boring. It looked like making friends at church wasn't going to be any easier than making friends in our neighborhood.

After church I clumped up to my bedroom to change clothes. I sat on my bed and stared at the only other two things in the room: my neatly closed suitcase and my music box.

I picked up the music box and studied the two glass girls on top. One girl was swinging and the other girl was pushing her. Dawn had given me the music box years ago. I liked to think that one of the girls was her and the other, me.

"I was real brave two days in a row, Dawn," I said aloud. "I spoke to real Chinese people in Chinese. I don't know if they understood or not, but I did try. Maybe one of these days I'll even be brave enough to dive off the high dive like you do."

I twisted the base of the music box and listened to the chimes play "You Are My Sunshine." How many times had Dawn told me I was *too* careful? Well I'd surprise her. I'd start being brave right now, and in four years I'd be so brave she wouldn't even recognize me.

The chimes plinked to a stop and I wound the box up again. I would make new friends in Taiwan, but I'd always need Dawn. No one could take her place. She didn't have to worry about that.

But suddenly I had a worry of my own, a new one. Four years was a long time. After four years would Dawn still want to be my friend?

Chapter Four
From the Middle of Nowhere

My watch read 5:58 when my eyes blinked open Monday morning. It was the first time I'd slept past five since we'd arrived. Now I understood what jet lag was. It was being so tired you couldn't see straight at seven in the evening, and wide awake at the crack of dawn. Sleeping that late was a good sign. Maybe I was almost through with jet lag.

I turned to look at the dress that lay neatly on top of the other clothes in my suitcase. "First day of school," the dress reminded me. Would the other sixth-grade girls wear dresses for the first day?

The alarm on Dad's travel clock buzzed. "Everybody up!" he yelled. "First day of school!"

I slipped on my dress, struggled with the zipper in back, and went to check myself in the bathroom mirror. I'll sure be glad when we get a full-length mirror, I thought. And closets and dressers and . . .

"Hurry up, Amy," A.J. said. "It's my turn."

I hurried.

Downstairs I found Dad cooking oatmeal. "Where's Mom?" I asked.

"Upstairs getting dressed. It's our first day of school too, you know. As soon as we drop you kids off, we're going to language school."

A.J. bounced down the stairs, three steps at a time.

Hud clumped down them one at a time, dragging his stuffed lion along by the ear.

Then Mom came racing down, clipping on her earrings.

"Mom, does my hair look all right?" I asked.

"Beautiful as usual. Listen, Amy, when you get to school I want you to help Hud find his classroom. Introduce him to the teacher. Make sure he knows her name. And help him find the bathroom. You know how he hates to ask."

"Sure, Mom."

"And A.J., try not to rip out the knees of your pants the first day, okay? And don't tease the girls too much. You may actually want them for friends someday."

"Yuck," A.J. said. "Mom, did you put my whole name on the registration thing this time?"

"Of course. But we told the principal you like to be called A.J."

"If the teacher calls me Adoniram, I'll die. Even if I tell her to call me A.J., the kids will never forget."

"Never mind," Mom told him. "Adoniram Judson Kramer is a good name. You should be proud of it."

"Is Hudson Taylor Kramer a good name too?" Hud asked. Mom assured him it was. I was just glad to be named after Amy Carmichael.

When we got to school, we spent several minutes looking around. Taichung International School wasn't anything like our neighborhood. It had a beautiful, large campus with plenty of trees and grass. It was the first grass I'd seen since we left America.

Hud wanted to explore the playground, but I told him we had to look for his classroom first.

We found his room and the bathroom and met the teacher. As I left, I heard her ask where he was from.

"Pinedale," he said.

"Where's Pinedale?"

I stopped to listen for Hud's answer. I knew he could hardly believe anyone wouldn't know where Pinedale was. It had been the center of his world since he was born.

"Pinedale's not too far from Hudson." Ever since he found out there was a town in Wyoming that was "named after him," he worked the town of Hudson into any conversation he could.

"And where's Hudson?"

"Above Rock Springs."

He had to get around to "Wyoming" before too long.

I left the elementary school building and went to find the one for middle school. We had visited the campus when we registered on Saturday, but as I walked, I studied it again. I passed the swimming pool and the tennis courts. I couldn't see the track, but I knew it was there just beyond a border of trees. If only Dawn were here to see how nice my new school was.

The best part, though, was the wonderful sound of English coming from every direction. I wouldn't have any trouble communicating here.

On the way to my classroom I saw Kelly standing by the seventh-grade door. She was talking to a classmate, but she waved as I went past. I hurried on to my own classroom.

When I got there, I found two girls whose hair was even a lighter blond than mine. They looked American, but they certainly weren't speaking English. It didn't sound like the Chinese I'd heard either.

"What's your name?" one of them finally asked me in English.

"Amy Kramer."

"Where are you from?"

"Pinedale, Wyoming."

They looked at each other a minute.

"Is Wyoming in the States?" one asked.

"Of course," the other answered before I had a chance. "The capital is Casper, remember? Fourth-grade geography?"

Some boys came up then, along with a couple of Chinese-looking girls who stayed to themselves.

After them came a girl who was definitely an American and looked like a model. One side of her long brown hair was pulled back just right to show earrings the same color as her eye shadow. I studied her out of the corner of my eye. She probably wouldn't notice an ordinary girl from Pinedale, Wyoming.

"Hi, Jessica," the two blondes called to her. The Chinese girls greeted her too. She said "Hi" to all of them and then turned to me.

"You're the new girl, aren't you?"

"Yes, I—I guess so. I mean I'm new this year."

"I'm Jessica Nyquest," she said. "I heard there was another American girl in our class this year. We had an American girl last year in fifth grade, but she went back to the States. She was my best friend."

Jessica told me that she was from Boston. Her dad was here with a sport shoe company. Her family would probably stay in Taiwan for only another year or two.

"Those two blonde girls were speaking some foreign language. Where are they from?" I asked.

"Hilkka and Riitta are Finnish. They're missionary kids like you. Then there's a Japanese girl in our class. Her name's Hisako. She's not here yet. Her dad's in business. Susan and Grace and Mickey are Chinese."

"Chinese? I didn't think Chinese kids could go to school here."

"They can if they have foreign passports. Susan and Grace were born in the States, and who knows how Mickey got her passport. If the Chinese have enough money, they can get them somehow. They want their kids to go to school here so they can learn good English and live in the States someday. Look—Mrs. Bronniman is here now so the door's open. Let's go in."

Jessica led me to the far side of the room near the teacher's desk. "Sit here," she said. "Teachers like kids who want to sit near them."

Jessica talked to me until class started, which kept me from feeling left out while everyone else visited with their friends. It sure was nice to have a friend right from the start.

Mrs. Bronniman started the class with introductions.

"As most of you all know, I'm Mrs. Bronniman," she said. "I come from the States, from Arkansas. And what is the capital of Arkansas, class?"

"Little Rock," everyone answered.

"Right. We have Kenneth Koh, who is new this year, from Malaysia. Where is Malaysia?"

"Just above Singapore."

"And we have—" Mrs. Bronniman leaned back against her desk and reached for a notebook to refresh her memory. "—Amy Kramer. Where are you from, Amy?"

"Pinedale, Wyoming."

"Does anyone know where Wyoming is?"

Whispers filled the room. Someone finally guessed. "Isn't it somewhere out by Colorado?"

"Correct."

Mrs. Bronniman had everyone else tell where they were from. There were students from the United States, Canada, Finland, Germany, Japan, Malaysia, and a sprinkling from China. The majority of the Chinese, although they had foreign passports, had lived most of their lives in Taiwan. Somehow, among all the places my classmates were from, Pinedale, Wyoming, county seat of Sublette County, sounded like the middle of nowhere.

Since this was English class, Mrs. Bronniman wanted us to write about what we had done during the summer. She said she would put our reports up on the bulletin board for everyone to enjoy.

Easy, I thought. This has been the most exciting summer of my life. I've traveled halfway around the world and now I'm living in a foreign country!

I knew that would sound great to Dawn back in Wyoming, but this wasn't a foreign country to the kids in this class. I would have to work hard to make it sound interesting. By the end of the class, however, all I had done was put the first teeth marks on my new pencil. I was glad when it was time to go to math class.

"I'll show you where Mr. Kulp's class is," Mickey offered. She was a Chinese girl with short hair who sat behind me during the first class. "My brother says Mr. Kulp's a hard math teacher."

"You don't have to bother," Jessica said. "I can show Amy around."

Wow. I'd been afraid I wouldn't have any friends, and now two girls were fighting for the chance!

I smiled. "You can both show me. That way I won't get lost for sure."

"Want some M&M's?" Mickey handed me a package. "Go ahead. I have another package in my lunch."

"Thanks," I told her. "I didn't even know you could get M&M's in Taiwan."

"Sure. My mom buys lots of them. We can have all we want. Wyoming's in the West, isn't it?"

"Yeah."

"Do they have cowboys and Indians there?"

"Uncle Pete's a cowboy. I mean he lives on a ranch and raises cows and horses. And we have lots of Indians, but they're just normal people. They don't wear feathers or live in tepees or anything."

"Does your uncle wear cowboy boots and a cowboy hat?"

"Sure. A lot of people do in Wyoming."

"Wow!"

While Mickey was busy exclaiming about "real cowboys and Indians," I heard someone yell from the playground, "Hey Adoniram Judson! Where's William Carey?"

I glanced over to see A.J. sticking out his tongue at the name-caller. The knees of his pants weren't torn yet, but they already had some pretty dark grass stains. It looked like I was doing a better job at making friends than he was.

Mickey sat in front of me in math class. That gave me a chance to study her shirt. It was an odd gold color. The back of it said, "Boy + Girl" in big letters. Then in smaller ones it said, "He is friendly and beautiful harmony in the countryside."

I didn't get it. I read it again. I still didn't get it. Why would anyone put such a weird saying on a shirt? I didn't have long to wonder, because Mr. Kulp started reviewing something the others had learned last year. It was all new to me.

After math, Jessica made sure she led me to science class and that Mickey got left behind.

"I don't understand what's written on Mickey's shirt," I told Jessica. "Am I missing something?"

"No. Mickey always wears stuff like that. Her mom buys her clothes, and her mom's English isn't that great."

"But why would anyone put words on a shirt that didn't make sense?"

"I can tell that you haven't been in Taiwan long," she said. "At least this time the words on her shirt are spelled right. You wouldn't believe some of the dumb things you see on clothes here. They use English words on things just for decoration. It's obvious that the people who design them don't know much English."

When we got to science class, Jessica chose two chairs for us that were surrounded by boys. I wondered why we didn't sit with the girls. Maybe Jessica wanted to be sure we didn't have any extra empty seats beside us.

"Is it Mickey?" I asked. But why didn't she want Mickey to sit with us?

Jessica glanced over to the other side of the room where Mickey was searching for a seat. "Look. I don't mean to gossip or anything," she whispered. "But, well, you have to kind of look out for Mickey. You may have already noticed that she's kind of strange. It's not because she's Chinese or anything. I mean, Susan and Grace are okay. But Mickey . . . "

Jessica cleared her throat. I figured she was looking for a polite way to describe Mickey. "I feel kind of sorry for her, you know. She's not really good at anything, including making friends. At first you think she's really nice because she's always trying to give you stuff. But don't let her fool you. She thinks she can buy friends that way. She's always trying to steal everyone else's friends."

I reached into my pocket and felt the bag of M&M's. The candies rolled into the cracks between my fingers like marbles in a sack. I had fallen for Mickey's tricks already. I was sure lucky to have Jessica to warn me about these things.

At lunch Jessica left to buy something at the student store. Mickey came and sat at the desk behind me.

"Want some potato chips?" she asked. She had a whole can of chips that looked as if they'd come straight from America. I could almost taste their saltiness. They sure looked better than the Chinese cracker things Mom had packed in my lunch. I started to reach for some when I remembered Jessica's warning.

"No, thanks," I told her. "I'd better eat what my mom sent me."

"I've been to Disney World. Have you?"

"We went to Disneyland last summer."

"Disney World is lots bigger. And it has Epcot Center. We went to Sea World too."

"Everyone's been to Disney World." It was Jessica, just back from the student store. "You should go to Singapore, Amy. It's clean and beautiful and everyone obeys the traffic laws. The weather's nice all year around. They have lots of stuff to see, and you can get really great bargains. My mom and I went there last year."

"Hong Kong is a good place to shop," Mickey said.

"Not as good as Singapore," Jessica told her. "And Paris is even better. We lived in Paris for two years before we came to Taiwan. Paris has all the latest styles. Asia is so backwards compared to Europe."

Mickey tried to tell me about Hong Kong, but I wasn't listening. All I could think about was the kids in class reading my report of the most exciting summer of my life. I was glad I had good penmanship. I'd have to come up with something really brilliant, or my handwriting might be the only part of my paper worth noticing.

Chapter Five
Chicken Feet and Shaky Knees

On Saturday, Aunt Martha and Kelly took our whole family to the market. Before we left, Dad gave each of us fifty NT to spend. NT stood for New Taiwanese Dollars, and Dad told us that fifty NT (NT$50) was worth about two American dollars. When Aunt Martha and Kelly arrived, Dad checked to make sure we each had our NT$50 safely tucked into our pockets.

"Oh yes," Aunt Martha said as we walked out the door. "You might want to know how to say 'thank you' in Chinese. It's *'sye-sye ni.'*"

A.J. laughed. "Sounds like 'shaky knees.'"

"Yes," she said. "It does sound a little like 'shaky knees.'"

Aunt Martha hunted until she found a parking spot three blocks down from the market. One by one we squeezed by motorcycles and cars parked along the way. When we got to the market road, Aunt Martha took charge of Mom and Dad. Dad had a good grip on Hud's hand. Kelly led me and A.J. through at our own speed.

Dozens and dozens of tiny stalls lined both sides of that narrow road, and each stall sold something different. It reminded me of a gigantic yard sale.

A.J. studied a fruit stall at the beginning of the market. "Look at all the fruit," he said. "What's that green bumpy kind?"

"It's Buddha fruit," Kelly told us. "It doesn't taste like much." She went on to point out dragon eyes, litchis, mangoes, bell fruit, and star fruit. One kind of fruit had sharp points on it. Its putrid smell overpowered the smell of everything else around. Kelly told us those were durians, and though they smelled and tasted awful, they were very expensive. I was glad to see some apples and bananas.

At one place a plump Chinese lady sat on a tiny stool selling fish. Several kinds of fish, eel, and turtles swam around in pans by her feet.

A.J. reached down to catch an eel by the tail. "Look. They're still swimming."

"Sure," Kelly told him. "If they're swimming, you know they're fresh."

A.J. shook the water off his hands and leaned over to inspect the frogs. "These frogs are all tied together by one leg. Oooooh. Look! Some of them have their guts hanging out."

"I think I'll go look at the necklaces," I told them. "I want to get something for Dawn. Maybe if I send something nice to her from Taiwan, she won't worry about me so much." Well, I hoped she was worrying about me.

A.J. ran to another stall. "Wow! Look at these space guns." He pulled the trigger and the gun started flashing colored lights and making weird sounds.

"A.J., try to act civilized," I said.

"How much is it?" he asked Kelly. She asked the seller in Chinese.

"Sixty NT," she told him.

"But I only have fifty." He dug a NT$50 bill out of his pocket and waved it around.

The man told Kelly something.

"He says since you're such a cute American he'll give it to you for fifty," she translated.

"Cute, ugh." But A.J. handed the man the money. "Shaky knees." He aimed the gun at him and pulled the trigger. The man just laughed.

We dodged motorcycles and pushed through crowds as we visited the endless line of stalls that sold everything from mothballs to American sewing machines. Some sellers yelled advertisements from blaring loudspeakers.

I looked for something for Dawn at a toy stall. I didn't see anything she'd like, but I did find a rubber band jump rope for NT$10. If I had my own jump rope, maybe it would be easier to get our Chinese neighbors to play with me. I decided I'd try to get something for Dawn for NT$40 and spend the rest on a jump rope.

We rounded a corner and went into a big building with open sides. The bottom floor was filled with stalls selling meat. A new smell attacked our noses.

A.J. pinched his nose shut. "Pew. It stinks in here."

"A.J., quit it," I said. "That's rude."

"But it does stink."

"She's right, you know," Kelly told him. "If a Chinese kid held his nose, no one would notice. But since you're an American, people will see and remember everything you do. Since they think that almost all Americans are Christians, they'll think that's how Christians act. When you think about it, holding your nose isn't a very polite thing to do."

A.J. didn't say anything, but he stopped pinching his nose. A.J. never meant to be rude; he just didn't think about manners much.

"How can you tell what kind of meat it is when it's not labeled in a package?" I asked Kelly.

"See those feet on the counter? You can tell they're pigs' feet." She looked around a little. "And there's the pig's head hanging from that hook. Of course it's just the skin, but you can still tell it's a pig."

A.J. pointed to some stuff hanging above the stall. "Look, there's his guts. Amy, maybe you can send Dawn some pig guts."

"She wouldn't want to do that," Kelly said. "Pig intestines are expensive and she only has NT$50." She grinned, but A.J. just went on gawking.

"Oooooh. There's the heart and brain and liver."

"The organs are the most expensive part," Kelly told us.

I saw Mom and Dad ahead and ran up to meet them. This grocery shopping was getting to be too much for me.

"How do you like the market?" Dad asked me.

"It would be better if I didn't have to go with A.J.," I said. "I see all the pretty things, but A.J. doesn't care about anything that's not sickening."

Aunt Martha was buying chicken from a chicken stall. I asked her why the chickens under the counter were still alive.

"It keeps them fresh," she said. "The Chinese are very particular about having fresh food. Some ladies even buy the chickens live and take them home to kill themselves. I prefer to have them do the killing, however."

"And why do those dead chickens still have their heads and feet on? They took the feathers off, so why didn't they chop the heads and feet off, too?"

"They do for me, Amy. And then they charge me a little less. Because we're Americans we don't care for the head and feet."

"You mean they eat—" I coughed. "Never mind. I don't want to know."

I hurried ahead to a flower stall. It had roses and lilies and a lot of flowers I couldn't name. I stooped down to smell some tiny yellow orchids, but all I could smell was the pork stall next door.

Tired of smelling dead animals, I pushed my way through the crowd to a new section.

At a jewelry stall I found a necklace with a tiny prism on it. I held it up to the sunlight and watched it sparkle. Dawn would love it.

"Forty dollars," the seller said in slow English.

I dug my NT$50 bill out of my pocket and handed it to her. She gave me a NT$10 coin for change and put the necklace in a little bag.

"Shaky knees—I mean, *sye-sye ni,*" I said.

She smiled and stroked my long blond hair.

Wouldn't Dawn be surprised to see how brave I was, buying her a gift in Chinese all by myself?

Then I noticed a toy stall farther down and pushed through the crowd to hunt for a rubber band jump rope. The seller had one, and when I held out the NT$10 coin he took it and put the jump rope in a bag.

Proud of myself for making two purchases without help, I hurried back to show Kelly and A.J. I pushed past a little truck loaded with watermelons and around a pot filled with sizzling-hot cooking oil. At the corner I turned back toward the enclosed area with the pork stalls. But it wasn't there. Was it a different corner I'd come around? I didn't remember that one-armed man selling bananas or those wind-up toys. But then my stomach had been objecting to the pork stalls and I hadn't noticed much.

I pushed through faster, desperate to find my family and Aunt Martha and Kelly. But the farther I went, the less familiar things looked.

"A-tok-a! A-tok-a!"

I rounded another corner and rushed down that road, but I knew I'd never been there before. I searched in every direction but I couldn't spot any Americans.

I was lost. I didn't know where my family was. They didn't know where I was. And I couldn't speak a word of Chinese—not any word that would help me.

I heard it again. *"A-tok-a! A-tok-a!"*

I turned around and elbowed my way through the crowd, trying to retrace my steps. But all the stalls looked alike. Had I seen that fruit stand before, or did it just look the same? How would I ever find my parents? "Lord, please help me!" I cried silently. I walked and walked, and finally I forgot that I was eleven-and-a-half years old and burst into tears.

"A-tok-a!" They were yelling at *me*. I just knew it. Why did they have to yell at me *now?* Weren't things bad enough? The last thing I needed was someone yelling at me in Chinese.

I slowed down to let another truck pass and got shoved against a cage of live chickens. I began to sob. Things couldn't possibly get any worse.

Then a brown Chinese hand grabbed my arm.

Chapter Six
Pointy Noses, Slanty Eyes

I tried to yank my arm free from the grip of that Chinese hand. But the more I pulled, the tighter the grip became. By now, I was packed into the middle of a thick crowd. Running was impossible.

Slowly I turned to face the person who held my arm. A wrinkled Chinese woman smiled up at me. She loosened her grip.

"Mama. Papa," she said, pointing down the road. I searched the scene before me but saw no sign of them.

She motioned for me to come, not with her hand and fingers turned up like we do in America, but with her fingers turned down.

"Should I go with her, Lord?" I prayed.

Surely this little old Chinese lady wouldn't hurt me with all these people around. I followed her down the road, around a corner, down an alley, down another road. All along the way people called to her. Finally we turned a corner and there stood my family with Aunt Martha and Kelly, all looking very worried.

"Sye-sye ni," Aunt Martha told the lady enthusiastically. My parents echoed their thanks.

I rubbed the last tears out of my eyes. *"Sye-sye ni,"* I told the lady. She smiled, stroked my hair, and handed me a beautiful red apple from a nearby fruit stall.

Mom and Dad and Aunt Martha all talked at once, asking me if I was all right and scolding me for getting lost. A.J. tried to say something to me too. Meanwhile, Chinese people chattered around us. It was too noisy to follow what anyone was saying. Then in all the confusion, one word stuck out like my own blond hair in a Chinese crowd.

"A-tok-a," someone said.

"What does that *'A-tok-a'* word mean?" I asked Kelly. She was about the only person who wasn't trying to tell me something.

"It means 'pointy nose' or 'big nose,' " she said.

As if being lost wasn't bad enough, now the Chinese had to make fun of the way I looked. I'd never thought my nose was all that big. I reached up to touch it.

Kelly laughed. " *'A-tok-a'* is just their way of saying 'foreigner.' Chinese people have flat noses, and most foreigners have pointier noses, so that's what they call us."

Foreigner. I felt like one, too. And what in the world was I doing in this terribly foreign country?

When we got home from the market, I found a book to read and went to my room. Other than school, I decided I wasn't going anywhere that I didn't have to—not for a good long time.

Several days passed before I wanted to even think about the market again. Then I was ready to write to Dawn about it and send her the necklace I had bought. I decided I wouldn't tell her about getting lost. I didn't want her to worry.

Dear Dawn,

How are you? I miss you! I've been in Taiwan for less than two weeks, but so much has happened already.

First of all, this necklace is for you to remember me by. I bought it at the market all by myself in Chinese! I wish you could see the market. It looks like one huge garage sale. You can buy anything there. Well, not chocolate chips or peanut butter, but you can buy them at special stores. They just cost a lot more. Taiwan has all kinds of fruits that I've never even heard of. I didn't know what half of the food at the market was.

It's really different here. You know how I told you I thought Taiwan would be a lot like California? Big cities and lots of people? Well, the cities are big, but not in the same way. I can't explain it. Everything is just so different from America.

I think I'll learn a lot here. I can see how Chinese people live, and I'm going to learn to speak their language. I don't know much so far, but I'm just getting started. I've spoken to several Chinese people. You wouldn't believe how brave I've been.

Of course I don't like ALL of the differences. Some things aren't as fun here. But I keep reminding myself that I'm not here to have fun. Missionaries win souls, and there's plenty of them to win. Amy Carmichael was brave and I will be too. Really.

Don't worry about me. I already have a few friends, but you'll always be my best friend.

Next time I'll tell you about my school and the church and our neighborhood. Write soon.

Your best friend forever,

Amy Carmichael Kramer

Writing Dawn made me feel better about living in Taiwan. I still wasn't ready to try making friends with the neighbor girls again. I needed a few days to work up some courage. But I decided I'd use my after-school time that week to learn the words to "Jesus Loves Me" in Chinese. Then next Sunday I'd at least be able to sing one song.

I got Kelly to teach me. She wrote the words down in letters from our alphabet instead of Chinese characters, so I could work on them by myself. The chorus went like this:

Ju Ye-su ai wo.

Ju Ye-su ai wo.

Ju Ye-su ai wo.

You sheng-jing gau-su wo.

After I knew the words pretty well, I decided to teach them to A.J. and Hud. Hud tried, but he couldn't remember any more than *"Yesu ai wo."* I told him that with those three words he could at least sing most of the chorus. A.J., however, wasn't interested. "I could sing 'Jesus Loves Me' when I was two," he said.

I knew what the problem was for A.J. Learning a song in Chinese wasn't daring and it wasn't funny. A.J. would jump from the moon if you dared him to. And he'd do anything for a laugh. Like the time he told someone in a church we visited before coming here, "People in Taiwan don't wear any clothes. We won't wear any either because it would offend the natives." The poor lady had looked like she'd swallowed a fork sideways. No wonder that church had never supported us. But A.J. hadn't meant anything by his comment—he just wanted to be funny.

Sunday came. I was feeling pretty good about being the first one in my family to sing a whole song in Chinese for church. My parents would be so proud. I might not be as brave as A.J., but I could be responsible.

At Sunday school when two girls pointed at me and giggled, I practiced my Chinese on them. *"Ni hau ma?"* I said. They just giggled and sat down.

I tried my greeting on several other girls. Finally one answered, *"Hau."* When I sat down, she sat next to me. A bookmark fell out of my Bible and she picked it up for me.

I knew what to say. *"Sye-sye ni."*

She smiled.

I tried to think of something else I could say to the Chinese girl. I had learned a few words in Chinese class at school. But I didn't have any reason to say the days of the week, or "pencil," or "book," or "banana." The only other thing I knew how to say was "good-by." I'd have to save that one for later.

A Chinese lady led the songs. Each time she announced a song, I held my breath to see if it was "Jesus Loves Me." Each time they sang something else. But Aunt Martha saved the day. When she got up to give the lesson, she had them sing a song first. "Jesus Loves Me." I guess she knew I'd been working on it.

I started out singing loudly and clearly on the first note. Some of the Chinese kids turned to stare, but not at me. A.J. was singing even louder and clearer, and off-key besides! All the time I had been trying to teach the song to Hud, he'd been learning it too.

What was he trying to prove? A.J. had always been better at sports than I was, but I got better grades. Was he trying to beat me at my own game? What did he think this was, a contest or something?

Maybe he was just trying to be funny. At least he'd learned the song—and it was my idea to do it. Things were going great. I had talked to a Chinese girl today. I had sung a song in Chinese. And now I had a plan for something else.

Before we left church, I asked Kelly for a Chinese kids' tract and a flier that told about the church services. I had her underline the place in the flier that told about Sunday school.

That afternoon after dinner I got out our badminton rackets. Actually the Petersons had loaned them to us until we got our things from America.

"I don't want to play badminton. It's too hot," A.J. said.

"Fine. I didn't expect you to play."

"Then who are you going to play with?" he asked.

I just shrugged and stepped outside. Neatly folded in my back pocket was the tract and the church flier. I put one racket by the side of the road. With the other, I gently bounced the birdie up and up again; every time it came down, I counted a successful hit. At first I could only hit it a few times before the bird dropped to the ground.

I was getting about ten hits in a row when a Chinese girl strolled out of the house next door. She stopped to watch me. It was Mr. Hwang's daughter. I thought she might be one of the girls I had tried to talk to in Chinese.

I picked up the racket I wasn't using and held it out to her. She took it right away. It was a good thing I'd chosen badminton instead of jump rope. It was pretty hard to jump rope with only two people.

We batted the bird back and forth. She'd serve it and I'd miss it. Then I'd serve it and she'd miss it. After a while we even returned it once or twice before it hit the ground. Of course, it wasn't a real game, and we didn't keep score. But I was playing, really playing, with one of our neighbors.

It would have been nice to be able to say something like "Wow" or "Good hit!" or "Oops" or "The wind blew that one. It wasn't your fault." But still, we were playing.

After a while I started to get bored, especially since we missed most of the time. The neighbor girl looked comfortable enough. I was dripping with sweat. Maybe badminton wasn't a good summer game in Taiwan. But my plan wasn't finished yet. I put down my racket and wiped the sweat off my forehead. I pulled the tract and the flier out of my pocket and handed it to her. She looked confused.

"Lai." I pointed to the place on the flier that told about Sunday school. *Lai* meant 'come' in Chinese. *"Lai, hao pu hao?"* (Come, okay?)

She nodded her head and wandered off.

I couldn't believe it. I had invited my first person to Sunday school—in Chinese. Maybe she would come and get saved.

I took the rackets in and poured myself a glass of cold water. Even after drinking it, I was still hot.

"Mom, can I have a *poki*?" I asked. *Poki* was a brand of Chinese popsicles.

"I guess so. Why don't you give one to each of your brothers, too?"

Hud and I sat at the kitchen table, and A.J. took his *poki* outside.

Hud took a few sucks. "What kind of *poki* is this?" he asked. "It doesn't taste orange."

I sucked mine. "I don't know. It doesn't taste like peach or apricot, either."

Mom grinned. "Where's your imagination? We're in an exotic foreign country now. It could be mango or kumquat or passion fruit. Maybe it's pomegranate."

I didn't know what a pomegranate was, but it sounded more exciting than orange. I'd used my Chinese three times today. A pomegranate *poki* was a good way to celebrate.

Pages rustled as Dad finished reading his paper in the living room. He came in to join our party. "Hey, where's the pomegranate *pokis*?" he asked.

A.J. came back in, slamming the front door. "Hey, Amy, Mom told us not to waste tracts and stuff," he yelled. "Tracts cost money, God's money, and we aren't supposed to waste them."

"I didn't waste any. I got a tract and a flier at church this morning, but I didn't waste them."

"Oh yeah? Then what are these?"

A.J. held out the papers I had just given our neighbor girl. They had been folded into neat paper airplanes and had crash-landed into the dirt.

My celebration was over.

Chapter Seven
Peanut Butter Friends

On Monday I was glad to go back to school and be just a kid. Maybe some day I'd get to be good friends with the neighbor girls. But right now I couldn't figure them out.

My school friends weren't all American, but they spoke my language and they did things the way I was used to. They were normal and predictable and good to be around, just like peanut butter. Peanut butter friends. That's what I'd call them.

We'd had two weeks of school already, and so far it was going great. With Jessica as my best friend, making more friends was easy. And having friends made everything easier—most of the time. Science class that day did make me wonder.

"Today we're going to study a fascinating animal called *Lumbricus terrestris.*" Mr. Hoffman made the announcement with the air of a circus ringmaster. His curly hair and baggy lab coat, however, made him look like a clown. "I want you to divide up into groups of two. Then I'll give each pair of you a *Lumbricus terrestris* to examine."

From across the table Jessica said, "You go with me."

I nodded. But then I glanced around to see who the other girls were choosing. Grace, Susan, Hilkka and Riitta sat at one table and formed teams. Mickey sat beside me, and Hisako sat on Jessica's other side, diagonal from Mickey.

"Jessica, will you be my partner since you're next to me?" Hisako asked.

"No. I'm going to go with Amy. You go with Mickey."

"But Mickey's too far away. Why don't you go with me, and Amy can be Mickey's partner?"

"Yeah," Mickey said. "Amy can be my partner."

"Amy's going to be *my* partner," Jessica said. "You switch places with Amy. Then you can go with Hisako."

"But I don't want to go with Mickey," Hisako whispered to Jessica.

"Amy doesn't want to be her partner either," Jessica whispered.

"Well, neither do I, and anyway Amy's closer to her."

"You can move," whispered Jessica.

Their whispers were getting louder. A deaf person would have had a pretty good idea of what was going on. I decided I'd better say something before it got any more embarrassing. "It's okay. I'll go with Mickey."

"But I want you to go with *me*," Jessica said.

"You go with Hisako this time," I told her. "I'll go with Mickey. It's only this one time."

Mr. Hoffman broke in. "All right. I see everyone has chosen a partner." He gave us a meaningful look. "I'll bring your *Lumbricus terrestris* around to you." He opened a jar, and a strong chemical smell filled the room.

Jessica tried one last time. "Amy, you trade seats with Hisako so she can be Mickey's partner."

Mickey answered for me. "No. Amy wants to be *my* partner, don't you?"

"Yeah," I said. "Jessica, you go with Hisako this time. Next time I'll be your partner."

Jessica leaned my direction and whispered, "You'll be sorry."

By now some of the boys had received the Lumberscuz terrawhatevers. They were dangling them in front of each other's faces and making the usual boy comments.

"Wow! Worms!"

"Pew! They stink!"

"That's the preserving solution you smell," Mr. Hoffman said. "By using preserved earthworms we don't have to leave the killing to inexperienced sixth-graders. After all, worms are God's creatures too. They deserve a little dignity."

One boy spoke up. "I've had experience, Mr. Hoffman. I've killed lots of worms."

Mr. Hoffman heard only what he wanted to hear. He didn't seem to hear the last comment.

"Look how long they are."

Mr. Hoffman heard that one. "They *are* long. They need to be big enough for us to examine their internal organs. That's another reason we're using preserved earthworms instead of digging for our own. With worms this size, we should be able to see their organs clearly once we cut them open."

"Cut them open? Oh, no!"

By now the girls were receiving their earthworms, and the comments were coming from them.

"I'm not going to cut a worm open. I'm not even going to touch it."

"One of us has to and it's not going to be me."

"It stinks. How can I cut it open when one hand is plugging my nose?"

When our worm came, I leaned back and let Mr. Hoffman put it in front of Mickey. At Uncle Pete's ranch in Pinedale I had dug for nightcrawlers lots of times. These worms, however, were smelly and slimy looking. Maybe I could get Mickey to do the dirty work.

Scott Rawlings was sitting behind Mickey. He turned around and held his worm in Mickey's face.

Mickey picked up our worm and dangled it back at him. "I'm not afraid," she said.

Mr. Hoffman called out above the hubbub. "The first thing I want you to notice about your earthworm is that it has no eyes or ears."

"Which end is his face?" asked Mickey.

"You can tell which end the head is on by finding the mouth. Worms do have mouths even though they have no eyes or ears. They are sensitive to heat, light, and touch, so they can find their way around quite well."

Mr. Hoffman pointed out the different parts of the outside of the worm. Then he passed out little knives. He taught us how to cut carefully through the worm's skin and pin it back to examine its insides.

The boys got their worms open right away. Most of the girls were still trying to figure out how to hold their worms without touching them. I didn't have to worry about it. Mickey was glad to do our dissecting. She sliced it right open and wiped the knife on Scott's T-shirt.

"Cut it out," Scott yelled.

"Why? Are you afraid?"

Mr. Hoffman ignored them and went on. "A short distance behind your earthworm's mouth you will find a small round object. It is the worm's brain. From the size of it, you can tell that earthworms are not the smartest creatures."

"Sounds like Scott," Mickey said.

"More like you," he answered. "Small brain. Can't see or hear. All mouth."

"I'm going to put my worm in your sandwich and make you eat it for lunch."

Mr. Hoffman chose to hear that comment. "No. We won't be eating these worms. Later on we'll eat mealworms. Mealworms are not true worms. Actually they're beetle larvae. And very nutritious. Of course they don't have much taste to them, but we'll fry them up with a little butter and onion and—"

"I'm not eating mealworms," Mickey said loudly. I imagined that when "Mealworm Day" actually arrived, Mickey would gobble up more than anyone else. Now I knew what Jessica meant when she said I'd be sorry for teaming up with Mickey. That's what I got for trying to be nice.

When the bell rang, the girls raced out of the room, eager to escape from the smelly worms.

"I sure am glad that's over," Hisako told me.

I agreed. Worms were bad enough, but I'd had to put up with Mickey besides.

A couple of hours later we had art class and it started all over again.

Even though we'd been in school for two weeks, this was our first art class. The first day of school was only a half day, and a school assembly had canceled art the second week. Art was my favorite subject, so I was glad we were finally starting it.

I liked the art room the minute I saw it. It was an orderly mess of bins, shelves, and cabinets all crammed full of art supplies. Brushes, paper, paints, and a thousand tools stuck out of containers everywhere. It was like going into an arts and crafts store after an explosion. It was a little disorganized, but it was wonderful stuff. I could hardly wait to get started making things.

Two giant work tables had been squeezed in between easels and boxes. Jessica sat on one side of me at the "girls' table." Mickey made sure she got the other side. I hoped art would go better than science.

"Wow. It looks empty in here," Riitta said to Hilkka as they found places around the table. "It sure looks different after Mr. Wu has cleaned out for the summer."

Empty? The only empty spot I could see was a strip of bare wall about a foot wide right next to the ceiling.

While we were finding seats and talking, a little Chinese man came bouncing out of the closet. His arms were loaded with sacks of macaroni of various shapes. "It's Mr. Wu," Jessica said.

Mr. Wu's thin black hair was all combed straight back. He kind of walked on his toes, which made him bounce even when he walked with a full load. He unloaded the macaroni bags on a counter and pushed his wire-framed glasses back up onto his nose.

"Well, the new sixth-grade class looks a lot like last year's fifth-graders." Mr. Wu leaned back on the counter and studied us carefully. "I see Travis is back from the States. Was it cold in Michigan, Travis?"

"Yeah, " Travis said. "I about froze my toes off. We got over a hundred inches of snow. It was great!"

"And did you build a snow man for me like you promised?"

"I built fourteen snow men last winter. I built one Chinese snow man for you. I took his picture but I forgot to bring it. Next week I will."

"You'd better. I'll be waiting. Hilkka, did your mom have that baby yet?"

"Yes," Hilkka said. "A boy. He weighed almost four kilos. His name is Jorma."

"Jorma. Good. A name I can pronounce right from the beginning. Now if he learns to paint like his sister we're in good shape."

Mr. Wu gazed from one side of the class to the other, continuing to size us up. "Let's see. We have a couple of new students." He checked his grade book. "Kenneth Koh and Amy Kramer." He looked up at us. "Kenneth and Amy, welcome to Taichung International School's best class."

A couple of kids groaned. "He says that every year," whispered Jessica. I just shrugged. I was tired of being "the new girl." After two weeks at Taichung International, I was ready to be one of the regulars. Still, I couldn't help liking Mr. Wu.

"Now. We'd better get down to business," he said. "For your first art project this year, I'm going to give you a choice. You can use clay to make a pot or pencil holder or some other useful container. Or you can make a genuine, authentic, wonderful, fantastic, awesome Chinese paper cutting, according to the time-honored custom of the oldest civilization on earth."

Jessica leaned over to whisper. "He always wants us to do Chinese art."

Mr. Wu showed us some paper cutting patterns we could do. There were some neat Chinese ladies, and some birds and flowers. My favorite was a tiger that stared straight at you no matter which way you looked at it. I could almost see that tiger on the wall above my bed. It would be perfect.

"What are you going to do?" Riitta asked Hilkka.

"A paper cutting would look good on my bedroom wall, but I could use a pencil cup too."

"I want to do paper cuttings," Mickey said to no one in particular. "I'm going to do the one with two birds."

Susan said, "A clay teapot would be nice if you glazed it red and black."

Grace nodded. "Yeah. Clay would be fun. But some of those paper cuttings really look good too."

"The birds and flowers would look good," Mickey put in.

"I like the tiger," I told Jessica. "The eyes look like he's looking right at you."

Jessica asked Hisako, "What are you going to do?"

Hisako shrugged. "I don't know. The Chinese ladies are pretty, but it might be hard to get the faces right. If you didn't get the eyes exactly right, it wouldn't look good."

"The birds wouldn't be hard," Mickey said.

Hisako asked Jessica what she was going to do. Jessica just ran her thumb across the teeth of her comb, bending the teeth back and forth with a zipping sound. Everyone waited.

"I don't want to do paper cuttings," Jessica finally said. "Anybody can cut paper from a pattern. With clay you can really make something—something you can use, not just a piece of paper."

Suddenly everyone's mind was made up.

Hisako agreed. "You're right. Anyway, it's hard to cut good eyes."

Hilkka decided she really did need a pencil cup.

Riitta agreed.

Susan guessed she'd do a clay teapot.

"A teapot sounds good to me," said Grace.

Mickey was clearly not moved by Jessica's reasoning. She said, "Let's do paper cuttings, Amy. You do the tiger and I'll do the birds."

"I don't know."

"I could *cut* in kindergarten." Jessica told me. She obviously thought paper cuttings were for babies. She continued thumbing the teeth on her comb. The noise was beginning to get to me.

Mickey began begging. "Come on, Amy."

"You can cut if you want," Jessica told me, "but the rest of us are going to be making real things. We'll be molding and glazing and firing. I don't want you to feel left out."

"Working with clay does sound like fun," I said. "Especially real clay that gets fired in the kiln. In Pinedale we only got to use real clay one time."

Jessica said, "You can cut paper at home."

Mickey tried again. "But you could hang the tiger in your bedroom or give it to your mother for her birthday or something."

Each girl looked at me. On our side of the room every sound ceased. Jessica even quit thumbing the teeth on her comb.

Why should they care if I made a teapot or a tiger? Yet their nervous stares told me that this was more than a decision about an art project. Jessica and Mickey were playing a very serious game of tug of war, and I was the rope.

From the looks of things, this wasn't their first tug-of-war battle. It probably wouldn't be the last. I sure didn't like this game. I twisted the ring on my finger round and round.

"I like the tiger," I said finally, "but Jessica's right. I don't get many chances to work with clay. I think I'll make a teapot."

Mickey crossed her arms angrily. "Well! I'm not going to be the only girl cutting. I guess I'll have to do clay like everyone else."

That left me wondering what in the world I was going to do with a clay teapot. So far I didn't even have a dresser to set it on.

Chapter Eight
The Impossible Choice

Two days later Mom met us at the door when we got home from school. Good news. The crate was coming that night. Soon we'd have all our things that hadn't fit in our suitcases.

A.J. whooped like a Wyoming cowboy and swung an imaginary lariat when he found out. "I'll get my cowboy hat and my boots. Uncle Pete says a cowboy without boots is like a prairie dog without a hole."

Hud asked, "What's a crate?"

I couldn't wait to see how my bedspread and curtains looked in my room.

"Oh. In all the excitement I almost forgot," Mom said. "Mr. Hwang brought some things over while you were at school." She looked around, mumbling about where she had put them.

I dropped my book bag. "I hope it isn't anything to eat."

"Not this time."

I sank into a chair. Tonight we'd get our things.

Mom pulled out the gifts. "Here's a tambourine for Hud."

"How do you work it?" he asked.

"You shake it or hit it on your hand."

Hud banged it on his hand and elbow and head and foot. He got the idea fast—unfortunately.

Mom shouted over Hud's banging. "And A.J., here's a popgun. It may not look like much, but if you do it right, it has quite a pop."

A.J. did it right.

"And here's something for you." Mom handed me a hair bow. Not an ordinary hair bow. On top of a big bow of sheer pink material was a red ribbon one and a plastic purple cat.

I stared at the bow for a few minutes, rubbing the scratchy pink material between my fingers. I searched my mind for something nice to say about it.

"I don't think I have anything that matches it," I called over the banging and popping.

"Not very many things would match it." A little smile tugged at the corner of Mom's lips. "It really was nice of Mr. Hwang to give it to you, though. How could he know what an American girl would like? Next time he comes out of his house, why don't you wear it outside and thank him?"

"But Mom, how can I thank him for something I don't even like?"

"You can thank him for being nice enough to think about you and get you something."

"I don't know how to say that."

"Just say, 'Sye-sye ni.' "

That was possible, I guessed, but I didn't want to think about it now with our crate coming tonight.

I grabbed my school stuff and headed up to my bedroom. With all the unpacking tonight, maybe Mom would forget about thanking Mr. Hwang.

Dad was waiting in my room with a new closet, a dresser, and a set of shelves. He knew I'd go crazy if our crate came and I didn't have a place to put things.

I hugged him so hard I knocked him off balance. "Thank you, Dad. It's just in time. Did Hud and A.J. get stuff too?"

"They got a dresser, but they'll have to wait on the other things. No problem. Not having things put away has never bothered them before. But their sister is another story. I mean, who else arranges her sock drawer according to primary color groups? I bet it took you fifteen minutes to decide where to put the white socks since they were a neutral color."

How did Dad know I'd struggled with the white socks? After all, I had only one sock drawer. Organized socks made it easier to get dressed. Dad chuckled, and I looked up to meet his smile.

I smiled back. "I just like things neat and tidy. I can't help it."

"No, I don't imagine you can." He yanked my braid. "It's not your fault. You get it from your mother. As long as you turn out as sweet as she is, the world will learn to live with you."

I had my clothes arranged by suppertime. Then around seven o'clock, a big truck ground to a stop out front, announcing the arrival of our precious crate.

The crate was huge, and there was no way the men could lift it off the truck. They pried off one side and began pulling out boxes. As fast as they unloaded the boxes, we stacked them on our living room floor until it was all one big happy mess.

I found my yellow and orange striped bedspread and scurried upstairs to try it on my bed.

Mom gathered pictures and knickknacks and looked around the house for places to put them.

Dad made a special "hands-off" pile for his tools.

A.J. discovered his kazoo. Too bad that couldn't have gotten lost.

Hud threw his toys into a big heap and then decided he liked his tambourine from Mr. Hwang better. He banged it on his knee and his hip and my elbow. He wore it on his head like a hat. Then he put it on his stuffed lion's head. "Don't worry, lion," he said. "Even though I have my other toys now, I'll always like you the best."

A.J. marched around the room buzzing out a song of some kind on his kazoo. Hud tossed his lion aside and marched after him, banging his tambourine.

Dad unpacked my flute and handed it to me. "Here's your flute, Amy, if you want to join the band."

"I think I'll pass."

Hud gave up trying to beat his tambourine to A.J.'s irregular timing. He found his Old Maid cards and sifted them through his fingers and into the tambourine with a sizzling noise. "Burn, burn, burn," Hud chanted.

"What are you cooking?" Mom asked, but he just started marching again.

I left the noise behind to organize my bedroom. The yellow and orange striped curtains were too small for our large windows. Maybe Mom could add some ruffles to make them wider and longer. I stacked games, belts, shoes, and other things into neat piles. I could put them away tomorrow when I had time to take care of them.

First I wanted to figure out where to put my knickknacks and posters. After all, the important stuff should come first. I found the perfect place for my parrot poster and the one with the monkeys. But the space over my bed needed something special. What could I put there? Something stuck in my mind: the tiger paper cutting. It would be perfect. But it was too late. I had already started molding a teapot that didn't match anything in my room. Even Mickey had started something out of clay.

So I had lost my tiger, and Mickey and I were both stuck with making things we didn't want. Why? Well, Mickey went along with the crowd, but I knew I'd chosen clay just for Jessica. That was all right. Sometimes you have to give in to make a friend happy.

"But what about Mickey?" a little voice inside me whispered.

"Mickey's not really my friend—at least not like Jessica is." But I couldn't help wondering how Mickey felt when no one ever wanted to do the things she suggested.

I thought about scenes from science class—and the earthworm incident. Being nice to Mickey could have its drawbacks. But the Bible said we should be kind to everyone. Maybe I could try a little harder to be nice to Mickey, just to make her feel better. Of course Jessica would still be my best school friend.

I moved my posters around again so there wouldn't be a blank space where the tiger should have gone. The new design was off balance and the colors didn't blend as well without the tiger, but it would have to do. I fastened them to the wall. By tomorrow night I'd have everything except the curtains in place, and my bedroom would finally look like it was mine. If I knew Mom, the house would soon be in order too.

Maybe then Taiwan could begin to feel a little like home.

On Friday we did a group project in geography. It sounded like fun—at first. Miss Johnson told us to divide into four groups. One group would draw a map of our room, the second would do the school campus, the third would draw a map of Taiwan, and the fourth would draw the world.

"Hisako, I want you in a group with Amy and me," Jessica said. "We need a good artist."

That sounded all right to me. In science class on Monday, Jessica had been determined to choose me over Hisako. Maybe Jessica's including her now would make Hisako feel better.

Susan and Grace formed a Finnish-Chinese group with Hilkka and Riitta. That left Mickey. Jessica might not want Mickey, but our group had fewer girls, so Mickey would end up with us anyway.

"How about going with us, Mickey?" I said.

Jessica punched me in the ribs with her elbow. "Amy!" she exploded in a loud whisper. "Don't you remember what happened the last time you teamed up with Mickey?"

I was sure Mickey had heard Jessica, but Miss Johnson broke in before anyone could say anything really nasty. "Good idea. Then each of the girls' groups will have four people."

Jessica crossed her arms, but she kept her voice soft. "Three is enough for our group. We just want to do the campus. If the other girls do the whole world, they'll need more people."

"But we already have four people," Grace protested.

I wondered if the girls had done group projects with Mickey before.

Miss Johnson's dark eyes stared into Jessica's. "Grace is right. I'm sure you girls will be glad to have Mickey, right?" It was a question with only one answer.

"I guess," Jessica finally said.

Voices babbled, and tables screeched while the groups rearranged the room. Huge sheets of paper slid onto tabletops. The hubbub of groups making plans filled the room and drifted out the windows.

"I'll draw the playground," Mickey offered when we had our paper all laid out.

"No. Let Hisako draw the playground," Jessica said. "Playgrounds are hard to draw, and Hisako's the artist. She can draw the elementary building too. Amy, do you want to draw the art-library-music building and the parking lot?"

"Okay."

"I'll do the swimming pool, the auditorium, and the sports fields," Jessica added.

"What'll I do?" Mickey asked.

"You can do the rocks by the gate," Jessica told her. "Don't mess them up, either."

As the hour wore on, Mickey kept drawing rocks and Jessica kept making her erase them. Finally, Jessica pointed to Mickey's eraser smudges. "Look. You erased a hole in the paper. Now we'll get a bad grade."

Mickey hurled her eraser to the floor and watched it bounce. She turned to Jessica. "If you think you're so good, you draw them. I quit. Anyway, I think your soccer field looks stupid."

"I knew this would happen," Jessica whispered to me. "Mickey never does her share."

Even though Jessica and Hisako liked my building and bushes, I was relieved to hear the bell ring for lunch.

Jessica grabbed her lunch and headed for the door without me. Sometimes we ate outside, but before this Jessica had always asked if I wanted to eat outside. Now she wasn't even waiting for me to catch up.

I wandered over to the steps where Jessica was eating and sat down quietly. She had already started her sandwich. She didn't bother turning my direction.

After I thanked God for my lunch, I took out my sandwich. "It's a nice day, isn't it?"

"It's okay."

"A little windy." I pointed to a plastic bag scooting across the grass. A boy ran after it. I took a bite of my sandwich, never tasting it.

Jessica said nothing.

Peanut butter glued my tongue to the roof of my mouth. When I had swallowed enough of it to talk straight, I asked, "Are you mad?"

Jessica crushed her juice box into a tight fist. "Look, Amy. If you want to be friends with Mickey, fine. But leave me out of it. I've known Mickey longer than you have. I know what she's like. And I don't want to have anything to do with her."

My throat was clogged by fear. I cleared it so a little bravery could trickle through. "Mickey's kind of strange. But she needs friends too. No one ever talks to her or does stuff with her. She's always left out. I don't want to be her best friend or anything. I just think it wouldn't hurt to be nice to her once in a while."

"Fine. You be nice to her. And while you're at it, find yourself another best friend."

"But I still want you for my best friend. You're much more my type."

"Make up your mind. It's Mickey or me. You can't have us both." She snatched up her lunch box and stamped away.

Chapter Nine
Invitation to Disaster

All weekend long I dreaded going back to school. What would I say to Jessica? She was trying to make me choose between her and Mickey.

Jessica included me, made me feel good, and made all the other girls like me. If only she would just be a little nicer to Mickey. Mickey didn't exactly fit in, but if Jessica expected me to be mean to Mickey, she was going to be disappointed.

I wasn't sorry for defending Mickey on Friday. But how could I calm the storm of Jessica's anger and make us best friends again? Had her anger disappeared since Friday, or had it become even stronger?

I prepared for the worst, but Jessica's anger seemed to have blown away over the weekend. Surprisingly, she was all smiles.

"I'm going to have a slumber party this Friday night," she told me. "No special reason. Can you come?" She explained all her plans for the big night.

I was sure Mom would let me go. She knew nothing about Jessica's blowup, and Mom wanted me to make friends. I could hardly wait to get home from school to ask her.

When I did, Mom didn't say yes right away. She put down the Chinese flashcards she had been studying. I could tell that she wanted to get all the details before she agreed.

"Who's going to this party?" she asked.

"The girls in our class."

"*All* the girls in your class?"

"Well, everyone except Mickey."

"Why wasn't she invited?"

"Mickey and Jessica don't get along too well. The truth is, Mickey doesn't get along with anyone. It wouldn't work for Mickey to come to the party."

"Jessica could have invited her. Then if Mickey didn't want to come, she wouldn't have to."

I shifted from one foot to the other. "You don't understand, Mom. If Jessica invited Mickey, Mickey would probably come, even though she knows Jessica doesn't like her. Mickey always pushes in where she's not wanted. Then she tries to bribe people into being her friends. Still, nobody really likes her."

"She must be lonely," Mom pointed out.

"I guess so. I do feel kind of sorry for her. Last Monday I chose Mickey to be my science partner. And Friday I invited her to be in our project group, even though the others really didn't want her. During science class she kept showing off and calling Scott names. And during our group project she blew up and refused to do anything."

Mom thought about that.

"It does sound like she has a problem," Mom admitted. "But her main problem may just be that she needs a little attention. It isn't easy being nice when you think no one likes you."

"I'll try. But it's Jessica's party. I can't tell her who to invite. Can I go? Please, Mom, please!"

Mom shuffled through the flashcards. "Mickey doesn't have to be one of your closest friends. But I'm not too crazy about a party where every girl in class is invited but one. Why don't you suggest that Jessica invite Mickey? If Mickey doesn't want to come, that's fine, but I think she should at least be invited."

"But Mom!" I protested.

Mom's look said, "That's final."

"Invite Mickey?" Jessica wailed when I suggested the idea. "Look, Amy. I told you. It's Mickey or me. If you want to be my friend, you've got to forget about Mickey."

"I know," I sighed. "I think you ought to be able to invite whoever you want. But Mom says I can't go to your party if Mickey isn't invited."

"Explain to your mom what Mickey is really like. That she acts up in class. That she sings off-key. That she's pushy. That she's a Buddhist."

"A Buddhist? Really? Maybe that would make a difference to Mom. I don't know, though. She surprises me sometimes."

Jessica frowned. I could tell her mind was busy making plans. Suddenly a light bulb clicked on in her brain and shone through her eyes.

"I know," she exclaimed. "I wanted to go swimming at the party, and this is ghost month."

"So?"

"So, Chinese don't swim during ghost month. They're afraid the ghosts will get them. Just tell your mom I can't invite Mickey because we want to go swimming."

"What about Susan and Grace? They're Chinese."

"That's different. Their families are Christians. They're not superstitious."

I knew I had Mom then. I couldn't wait to get home from school.

Hud chose this day to dawdle and poke all the way home. He's a smart little kid, interested in everything, but today I was in a hurry.

Several people were setting out worship tables along the way. That really slowed Hud down. The worship tables fascinated him, even though he had already seen tables like them several times. He had a million questions.

"Amy, what are they doing?" he asked.

"Worshiping."

"How come they're always worshiping?"

"I don't know."

"Mommy says they don't worship God. So who do they worship all the time?"

"I don't know. The ghosts I guess. It's ghost month."

"I thought there was no such thing as ghosts."

"Well, maybe not. But they worship their grandparents and relatives after they die. They don't know about the one true God in heaven. That's why we came to Taiwan, you know."

"To tell them?"

"Yeah."

"I think we better tell them pretty soon."

"We will—after we learn Chinese."

Hud eyed the different kinds of fruit on the tables while I tried to hurry him along. Whiffs of sickly sweet incense drifted into the air as we passed. One lady was holding a stack of faded yellow papers about the size of recipe cards. She dropped the papers a few at a time into a can of flames near the table.

"What is she burning?" Hud asked.

I had seen these fires several times during the past three weeks of ghost month. I thought Hud had too, but maybe no one had bothered to explain anything to him.

"They're burning money," I said.

His eyes grew wide with surprise. "Really?"

I chuckled. "It's not real. It's just spirit money. They think if they burn the spirit money, it will give their dead relatives something to spend in their afterlife, I guess."

"Is it American money or NT dollars?"

"I don't think it matters much when you're dead. Hud, I know this is interesting, but could we hurry along a little? I want to get home and ask Mom something."

Finally we got home. As usual, Mom was studying Chinese. Hud went into the kitchen for a snack, but I stayed behind to ask the big question.

"Didn't you say we should choose Christians for friends?"

She looked at me as if she suspected a trap. "Well, your very best friends should be."

"Mickey's a *Buddhist!* Her family worships idols and ancestors and everything!"

"That doesn't mean you can't be her friend."

I stared at Mom in disbelief. What would she come up with next?

"Amy, twenty million people live around us in Taiwan and most of them are Buddhist. Or Taoist, or Confucianist, or ancestor worshipers, or a mixture of them. We came to Taiwan to help these Buddhists become Christians. Do you really think they'll listen to us if we refuse to be their friends? We plan to build friendships with lots of Buddhists. Mickey's no different just because she goes to an English-speaking school."

"Oh, that," I said. "Sure I know we have to be friendly to Chinese so that they'll want to be saved. I don't mean that kind of friend. I mean, you know, the kind of friend you stay overnight with and do a lot of stuff with. The kind of friend you have because you like each other and you enjoy doing things together. You taught us to be careful who we chose to be that kind of friend, right?"

Mom put her Chinese book down and thought a minute before she answered.

"Well, yes. We should be careful who we choose for our close friends because what they say and think and do will have a big influence on us."

"See? Mickey's a Buddhist, and all she cares about is getting attention."

"Maybe so. But she also needs a friend. If you can be a true friend to Mickey, you can show her what being a Christian really means. Even Christian friends can be bad for you if they care more about themselves than the Lord. For that matter, do you really know for sure that your good friend Jessica is a true Christian?"

I twirled my hair round and round my finger. "Well, she . . . uh . . . her family goes to the English community church on Sundays, at least when they're in town. Jessica said Susan and Grace are Christians. She wouldn't say that about someone if she wasn't a Christian herself, would she?"

"Lots of people call themselves Christians who have never really asked Christ to save them. And lots of people say they believe the Bible. But that doesn't mean they're sorry for their sin. Or that they're counting on Jesus' death on the cross to pay for their sin. Even in America, not very many of the people who go to church and say they believe the Bible are true Christians. You know that."

I nodded slowly. "Okay, I don't know for sure if Jessica's a Christian." What was the other argument I'd had about the slumber party? I started a braid in my hair. Something else Jessica had said about Mickey. Oh, yes.

"At least Jessica's family believes the Bible." I had to defend my friendship with Jessica somehow. "Mickey's family is very superstitious. Jessica wants to go swimming, and this is still ghost month. Chinese are afraid to swim during ghost month and Mickey is Chinese. So can I go to the party?"

Mom frowned at me and heaved a big sigh. "I guess so." She ruffled the pages of her Chinese book. "But listen. This Mickey sounds lonely. Do you girls ever play with her?"

"Mom. We're in the sixth grade. Nobody 'plays.' "

"Okay. Do you ever talk to her? Laugh at her jokes? Include her in the group when you do whatever you do?"

"I try, Mom. But it's hard. Mickey just doesn't fit in."

"Maybe she could fit in if you'd get the other girls to give her a chance."

"Mom! I can't fight the whole sixth grade." I rubbed my forehead. It was beginning to hurt. "The other girls have known Mickey for years. They know what she's like. She's not their type and she's not mine either. I promise I'll be nice to her. But you can't expect me to be too friendly to her, or I'll lose all my other friends. I try to pick the kind of friends that are good for me. I just don't think Mickey is that kind of person."

Mom sighed again and looked down at her Chinese book. Then she looked up at me again.

"All right," she said. "But don't forget that the Bible says Christians are supposed to be different—and one of the things that makes them different is kindness. God wants us to be kind to people who aren't especially popular and lovable. You know what I mean?"

"Sure, Mom. I'll see what I can do."

Hud marched into the room just then. He carried the tambourine filled with the same Old Maid cards. "Ssssss," he hissed. "Burn, burn, burn."

"What are you cooking this time?" Mom asked him.

Hud just shook his head. He grabbed some of the cards and let them drop through his fingers back into the tambourine. His actions reminded me of something. If only I could remember what. My little brother circled around the room and left. "Burn, burn, burn," he said.

Then I remembered. "Mom. Hud isn't cooking. He's burning paper spirit money!"

Mom gasped and ran after Hud. I headed for my room.

So Hud was playing spirit worship and Mom wanted me to be friends with a Buddhist. On the way upstairs I pushed

Mom's talk to the back of my mind and thought about the strange things this country was doing to our nice Christian family.

Chapter Ten
An Unworkable Puzzle

Life was a big puzzle these days. How could I keep everyone happy? Jessica wanted to be my friend, but she insisted I ignore Mickey. Mickey wanted to be friends, but she always wanted me to do something different from what Jessica wanted me to do. Mom wanted me to be friends to both of them. It was like trying to fit two different jigsaw puzzles together.

Mickey was the impossible piece that refused to fit into the picture. I would be friendly to her, of course, but maybe I didn't exactly have to be her friend. With twenty million other Chinese around, why should I have to treat her so special? Since school had started, I'd almost forgotten about the neighbor girls. What could I do to make friends with them?

I wandered around my room looking for ideas, until I found my rubber-band jump rope. I had bought it over two weeks ago to use in making a Chinese friend. This was a good time to try it out.

I changed into play clothes, stuck my jump rope into my pocket, and headed for the door.

As I sat by the door putting on my tennis shoes, I could hear Chinese kids outside. *"A-tok-a, a-tok-a, a-tok-a."* That meant A.J. was outside.

A.J. answered them. "Slanty eyes, slanty eyes, slanty eyes." How embarrassing.

I slipped outside and saw the Chinese boys busy at a game of keep-away. A.J. dashed between them and made a wild grab at the ball, trying to get in the game. The ball bounced around and over him several times as he tried to get it.

I ignored them. Three girls squatted in the street eating dry instant noodles straight out of the bag. I crept up to them and squatted down beside them.

"Ni hau ma?" I asked.

They stared at me, giggled, and went on eating.

"Do you want to play?" I asked them in English, holding out my jump rope.

One of the girls tried to copy me. "Jewan pray?"

They giggled some more. I didn't know what to do next. Finally I stood up. My legs were beginning to hurt. How could they squat like that for so long?

Suddenly one of the girls stood up and grabbed my jump rope. I thought it might be Mr. Hwang's daughter, who lived next door. She tied it into a loop. Then she and another girl put it around their ankles while the third began to jump. I had played "Chinese" jump rope back in Pinedale. This game was a lot like that. I watched them carefully so I would know what to do.

The first jumper made a mistake and was counted out, so the Hwang girl took her place. When she missed, the last one began to jump. I figured my turn would come next, but I was wrong. The three girls kept taking turns, leaving me out completely.

"Can I jump?" I finally asked, pointing to myself.

The Hwang girl, who was holding the rope, slipped it off her ankles. She motioned for me to take her place.

I wanted to jump, not hold the rope, but since I couldn't tell them that, I just held it anyway. After each girl had taken several more turns, one of them pointed to me.

Since I couldn't speak Chinese, the girls called out the steps while I jumped into the rope. I did it just like I'd seen them do it. At least I thought it was the same. But suddenly they started yelling and pointing at me. One of the girls who was holding the rope slipped out of it and motioned for me to hold it.

How could they count me out when I didn't even know what I'd done wrong? I didn't even get my fair share of turns.

I was glad when Mr. Hwang came out of his house, mumbled some Chinese at me, and motioned for me to follow. He brought A.J. along too. When we got inside, he handed each of us a can of something and a plastic spoon.

A.J. read the English part of the label. " 'Mixed congee.' I wonder what it is."

I smiled, told Mr. Hwang *"Sye-sye ni,"* and turned to leave. He stopped me, reached out for my can of congee, opened it, and handed it back. He wanted me to try it.

I took a small bite. An itsy bitsy bite, to be exact. It tasted something like cold, very sweet pinto beans. I gulped it down and tried to smile.

Mr. Hwang opened A.J.'s can too. A.J. grinned at me. I knew the smile wasn't genuine. He dug his spoon in deep and shoveled a huge bite into his mouth.

"Delicious," he said, as if he were eating a hot fudge sundae.

Mr. Hwang grinned at A.J. and then he looked at me. He wanted me to eat some more. I wanted to tell him, "Look, Mr. Hwang, I'm sure you Chinese think this stuff is great, and it's very nice of you to offer. But I'm just not a cold congee person. I'm more of a peanut butter person." But it was hopeless. I couldn't explain it in Chinese, and even if I could, Mr. Hwang probably wouldn't understand. I took another itsy bitsy bite.

A.J. slurped another mouthful and patted his stomach as if it tasted wonderful.

I faked a smile at A.J. and said, "Quit showing off, A.J. This stuff is terrible and you know it."

A.J. grinned up at Mr. Hwang. "You're the hypocrite. If this guy knew English, you'd be in big trouble."

He took another big bite.

I glanced up at Mr. Hwang. He had finished watching our reactions and had begun to inspect his prize orchid which hung by the door. I decided it was a good time to go.

"We've got to be going now," I told Mr. Hwang, pointing at our house. He nodded and reached for his watering can.

Once inside our door I tossed the rest of my congee in the trash. Then I realized that the girls still had my jump rope. I went out to get it. But one look out the door told me it was too late.

The girls and my jump rope were long gone.

Chapter Eleven
Crossing the Pacific

I'd had my second bad experience with the neighbors, and once again I was glad to go back to school. At school everyone spoke my language. Nobody made me eat weird things. There were rules, and everyone followed them. Well, maybe not all the time, but at least we knew what the rules were. Trying to get along in my neighborhood was like trying to play Monopoly with the rules from chess.

Friday was party day for us girls, and we didn't let anyone forget it. Our suitcases and bags were heaped into a big pile at the back of the room. Plans for the party filled every break time. At lunch I barely tasted my sandwiches as Jessica told us about the kinds of pizza we'd be having that night. I—and everyone else—could hardly concentrate on school work.

Well, there was Mickey. She wasn't excited, of course. But she couldn't concentrate on her work either. She was mad. When the rest of us formed a circle to talk about the party, she didn't even try to butt in. I tried smiling at her a couple of times, but she just stuck her lower lip out and looked away.

Just before our last class that day I noticed Mickey going into the restroom. I could have waited until school was over, but I thought maybe I could say something to make her feel better.

I had my chance when we were both washing our hands. "I . . . I'm sorry it didn't work out for you to, uh, you know, come to Jessica's party. It's a swimming party, you know, and, uh, Jessica didn't think you could go swimming, you know, since it's ghost month and everything."

"Who cares about Jessica's dumb old party?" Mickey splashed water everywhere. "I wouldn't go to Jessica's party if she gave me all the M&M's in America. My mom's taking me to Taipei. We're going to stay in the Grand Hotel and eat at Pizza Hut and buy lots of clothes. We're going to the zoo and the National Palace Museum and—and—and who cares about your stupid party? I have better stuff to do!"

Mickey slammed the restroom door behind her.

It sounded like Mickey had plenty to do this weekend anyway, I thought. If she was really going to do all that.

The last hour of classes dragged on and on, but finally it was time to leave. The company that Jessica's father worked for provided a van for all the company kids at our school. We piled into it. With six extra girls it was kind of crowded, but we were too excited to care.

The van pulled into the gate of Jessica's compound, and I was in a whole different world. The houses were square and concrete, but other than that, they looked like American houses. No bars blocked the windows. Each house had a huge yard with green grass and a driveway. A big playground sprawled across one part of the compound, and I could see the swimming pool beyond that.

Inside Jessica's house I could forget that I was in a foreign country. Thick carpet spread over every floor, and American wallpaper covered the walls. The furniture was soft and comfortable. Most of all, it was cool. Every room was air-conditioned.

"Your house is really beautiful, Jessica," I said. "We just got our crate from America. Mom still doesn't have all the stuff arranged, and some of the windows don't have curtains yet. So it still doesn't look like much." But I knew our house would never look anything like this.

"Your mom sure is a good decorator," Susan said. "This house looks like it came out of one of those American home magazines."

"My dad's company provided a lot of the stuff. But my mom did a lot of work on decorating too," Jessica said. "She ordered stuff out of catalogs and had it sent from America."

"Doesn't that cost a lot?" I asked.

"Sure. But Dad doesn't care. He just wants Mom to be happy here. We have Sara Lee cheesecake. Anyone want some?"

How could we say no to an offer like that?

I promised myself I would take my time eating that cheesecake. I wanted to enjoy every bite. The other girls weren't used to cheesecake, so it was nothing special to them. When Jessica saw how much I liked it, she offered me a second piece while the rest changed into their swimsuits.

I nibbled off a piece of cheesecake and rolled it around on my tongue. "Sorry I'm so slow. But it's been so long since I've had cheesecake. I didn't know you could buy stuff like this here."

"You can get lots of stuff at Jimmy's," Jessica said. "It's over on the Harbor Road. Mom buys all our American food at Jimmy's. The rest she gets at the supermarket."

"Doesn't she ever go to the market?"

"You mean the open market?"

I nodded.

"Mom went there once. She hated it. She said she'd never go there again. It's just not sanitary. All the meat lying out in the open and everything. Mom would rather go to the supermarket where she can have a shopping cart and air conditioning."

I told Jessica about my experience at the market and how I got lost. And then before I knew it, I was telling her about the cold congee and how hard it was to make friends in our neighborhood.

"I tried to play Chinese jump rope with the girls," I said. "But they hardly ever let me jump. They counted me out when I didn't even know what I'd done wrong. They could have at least given me an extra turn. I'd never played it like they played it before, and I couldn't understand the steps they called out. Then when they left, they stole my jump rope!"

"I'm not surprised. You're in Taiwan now. Chinese know they can cheat you and get by with it because you're an American and you can't do anything about it. I'm sure glad I don't have to live in a Chinese neighborhood. Chinese people are so weird. Susan and Grace are okay. They're almost American. But normal Chinese—" she pulled on the pink heart that dangled from her ear, "—well, I like living out here with other Americans. Don't worry. I'll be your friend. We're too old to play jump rope anyway."

I realized, then, that with all my storytelling I had eaten my second piece of cheesecake without even tasting it. I knew it wouldn't be right to ask for a third piece.

We didn't swim long. Everyone wanted to come in and watch videos. Jessica's mom let us eat supper in the living room so we could watch videos while we ate.

Jessica carried a steaming pizza into the living room. "Mom made two big pizzas just for us."

"What about your dad?" I asked. "Doesn't he get to eat?"

"He usually eats out. He has a really important job so he has to work late. And then of course he travels. Hong Kong. Tokyo. Singapore. Bangkok."

I passed plates around. "I bet you miss him." Dad had been gone a lot of weekends during our three years of deputation. But I knew he had tried to spend as much time as he could at home. Jessica's dad sounded like he was gone most of the time.

"It's okay. It's rough having an important father who makes a lot of money, but we try to get by." She laughed. "This pizza is pepperoni. The Canadian bacon will be done in about twenty minutes."

We each took some pizza. I leaned back and held my piece up to my face, breathing in the sweet perfume of genuine American pizza. I blinked my eyes closed in a silent blessing. "Thank you for the pizza, Lord," I prayed. And I meant it with all my heart.

Jessica's grandparents in the States had just sent her a couple of videos with some really funny movies on them. While we watched videos and filled up on pizza, I thought about my own family. They were eating something over rice in a steamy-hot house. No trucks drove past Jessica's house blaring loud Chinese messages. I watched the latest Coke commercial from the States and pretended to be back in Pinedale.

The first movie we watched came off the Disney Channel. When the outline of Mickey Mouse flashed onto the screen, Hisako said, "Look. There's Mickey. And we thought we left her behind at school."

Jessica laughed. So did everyone else.

"They kind of do look alike, now that I think about it," said Riitta. "Both Mickeys have big ears."

Everyone laughed louder. I had never noticed that Mickey had particularly big ears. What would Mickey think if she could hear us? Mickey Mouse was cute, so maybe looking like him wasn't all that bad. Maybe.

"I don't know. I feel kind of sorry for Mickey." I took another piece of pizza and rearranged the pepperoni in neat rows. "It must have been hard for her—the only girl in class not coming to the party today."

Jessica slammed her Coke onto the coffee table so forcefully it almost spilled. "You know we couldn't have asked Mickey. This is a swimming party and it's ghost month. Chinese don't swim during ghost month."

Grace grabbed Susan's arm. "We're Chinese and we swim."

"You guys don't count. You're bananas," Jessica said. "Yellow on the outside. White on the inside."

Everyone grinned, even though we'd all heard the joke before.

Susan giggled. "You can call me a banana, an orange, or even a pineapple. I don't care. Just don't call me Mickey Mouse. All Chinese are *not* alike."

"Thank goodness for that." Hisako snickered. "Can you imagine living in Taiwan with twenty million Mickey Mouses?"

"Mickey's a little strange, but she's not all that bad, is she?" I asked.

"Believe me, Amy, she's that bad." Jessica took another piece of pizza. "You saw how she quit working on our group project just because I gave her some suggestions on how to draw her rocks. Imagine not knowing how to draw rocks! And then when I help her, she gets mad. Mickey is always getting mad."

I remembered my conversation with Mickey in the restroom. She had a temper problem all right.

"What I don't understand about Mickey," Jessica said, "is how she can be so weird and still brag all the time. I mean, what does Mickey have to brag about, anyway?"

The timer buzzed in the kitchen, and Jessica jumped up to answer it. "Hold everything. I've got to go check the pizza, but I'll be right back."

Susan spoke up. "Take Jessica's word for it. She knows what Mickey's like. Mickey can fool you at first. She fooled me. Mickey and I used to be friends when I first came to Taichung International in the third grade. And there was another girl who's in America now. Ann Tsai. The three of us used to do things together. Then in fourth grade Jessica came to school. She helped us to see how weird Mickey really is. Jessica can just tell things about people."

"Yeah. We owe a lot to Jessica," said Grace. "She was really popular from the beginning. She had lots of friends. But she made sure all the other girls played with Susan and me at recess. In fourth grade, recess is still a big deal. Jessica made sure we got counted in."

Hilkka licked tomato sauce off her lips. "And when Jessica counts you in, you're in."

"You're really lucky, you know," Hisako told me. "Jessica not only counted you in, she picked you for her best friend. When her best friend from last year went back to the States, we all wondered who she would choose this year. And you're the lucky one."

"Who wants Canadian bacon?" Jessica called as she carried in a steaming hot pizza. No one said any more about Mickey. I was glad.

After we watched videos, we went to Jessica's room and practiced doing hairdos on each other. Finally, about midnight, we rolled out blankets on the carpet and curled up for the night. Long after the other girls fell asleep, I lay awake thinking about cheesecake and pizza and thick carpets. It was a sweltering summer night in the middle of Taiwan. Yet here I lay, cool as a watermelon. It was almost as good as being back in America.

I learned something that weekend. Taiwan is a foreign country with a foreign language and foreign food. But a small piece of America hides inside that foreign country. You can find American schools and American restaurants and American-type stores in the Chinese city of Taichung. Some people live in a little American community in an American house. They drive through Taichung from one American spot to another, and they rarely see the real Taiwan, except through their car windows.

But my trip to America couldn't last forever. Late Saturday afternoon it was time to go home. As Jessica's driver drove us home, I felt as if I were crossing the Pacific Ocean, leaving America behind, and going back to my very Chinese neighborhood.

I said good-by to Jessica and the others and stepped out of the air-conditioned van. A ton of hot air slammed down upon me.

"Hallo, hallo, hallo," said a little Chinese kid practicing his entire English vocabulary on the lucky American.

Three other little kids joined him so that they could stare at me too.

A string of firecrackers exploded in a deafening racket, scaring me half out of my skin.

I was home.

Mom heard the commotion and came out from the kitchen to welcome me.

"What's all the firecrackers about?" I asked her.

"Just part of ghost month, I guess."

Ghost month. How could I forget? I dragged my stuff up to my room and flopped across the bed on my stomach. The room felt as hot and steamy as a sauna. I yawned. Last night's late talking must be catching up with me. I was just drifting off to sleep when Hud hollered up the stairs. "Amy, your friends are here!"

I could hear Chinese whispering at the bottom of the stairs. I pulled myself out of bed and glanced down the stairs. There stood the neighbor girls. When they saw me, they held up my rubber band jump rope, jabbered in Chinese, and motioned for me to come play with them. For weeks I'd been hoping that they'd come and ask *me* to play with *them* for a change. But not now.

I was dead tired. And after staying in Jessica's little America overnight I needed some time to get used to Taiwan all over again. The last thing I wanted was Chinese visitors.

As I clumped down the stairs, my only thought was how to get rid of them. I tried to think how to say "Get lost" in Chinese—in a polite way, of course.

"Bu yau," I mumbled sleepily. I had learned that in Chinese class at school. It meant "Don't want," as in "I don't want to," or "I don't want it" or "Leave me alone!" Those two words could come in real handy at a time like this.

They jabbered something in Chinese.

"Bu yau."

They jabbered something else.

"Bu yau."

They offered me my jump rope.

"Bu yau." I spoke louder this time. I didn't want the thing back. I didn't ever plan to use it again.

They tried to push the jump rope into my hands.

"Bu yau, bu yau, bu yau." I clasped my hands behind my back so they couldn't force me to take it.

They dropped my jump rope and left.

I fell back onto my bed and closed my eyes tight, determined to block everything but sleep from my mind. But it was no good. Those Chinese faces pushed their way between me and sleep.

Okay, maybe I hadn't been very friendly. But they couldn't have picked a worse time to come calling. And then they wouldn't take *"bu yau"* for an answer. Besides, I had tried to play with them before, and they didn't even play fair. Jessica said I was too old for jump rope—maybe she was right.

After this I'd still smile when I saw them. And maybe I could try taking them to Sunday school. But that was going to have to be good enough. How could I expect to be friends with them anyway, when I couldn't even speak their language?

I punched my pillow to rearrange the lumps. Those Chinese kids had their own friends and I had mine. I had peanut butter friends. Comfortable, understandable, predictable peanut butter friends.

And if my school friends were peanut butter friends, what were the neighbor girls? They were just chop suey. I could get along fine without them. Even though I had to live in a foreign country, I was learning how to make it more like America.

I yawned. Maybe Taiwan would finally start to feel like home.

Chapter Twelve
Chop Suey Problems

They stood glaring at me with frowns on their faces: Mr. Hwang and the neighbor girls and the lady who found me in the market. Mr. Hwang held a can of cold congee in one hand and a gun in the other. It was only a green squirt gun, but he held it like a deadly weapon, filling me with unreasonable terror.

"Eat this or die!"

I could understand what he said, but somehow I knew he wouldn't understand me. None of them could understand me. I wanted to tell them I didn't like cold congee. That it was nothing personal. That very few Americans would like it. But I didn't know how to say that in Chinese.

I stood staring at Mr. Hwang, trying to think of some Chinese words to say. *"Ni hau ma?"* I tried.

Mr. Hwang crept closer and closer, his squirt gun centered at my chest. He pulled the trigger. Bang! He shot and shot and shot. Would he never quit?

I clutched my chest and thrashed wildly until the sheets came untucked and wrapped around my legs. I could barely move. Still the gunshots rang out. But no. It wasn't gunshots. It was firecrackers.

A dream. Just a dream and those horrible Chinese firecrackers exploding outside my window. Was this the last day of ghost month? Or did they have another reason for the explosions? I didn't know and I didn't care. I was sick of firecrackers.

I tore off the sheets and leaped to my window.

"Shut up, Chop Suey!" I yelled.

Mom opened my door and stuck her head into my room. "Was that you, Amy? Did you want something?"

"No. I mean, never mind. It was nothing."

"Sorry about the firecrackers, but it's about time to get up and get ready for church anyway."

I fell back onto my bed. Was that really me just now yelling out the window like a lunatic? What could have made me so angry? That crazy dream! Mr. Hwang, the market lady, the neighbor girls. I seemed to remember saying *"Bu yau"* a lot. Did I dream that too, or was that last night when the girls came to visit me? At the time *"Bu yau"* had seemed like a perfectly reasonable thing to say, but now it seemed a little unfriendly. I hoped they hadn't taken it the wrong way.

I shuffled to my closet. It was Sunday morning. That meant sitting through Sunday school and two church services in which I would understand nothing. Sweat trickling down my neck while I stared at my Bible. Chinese kids comparing my blond hair, light skin, and hairy arms and legs to their dark hair, dark skin, and bald bodies. One more day until I could get back to my peanut butter friends, American classes, and air conditioning.

I yanked out the coolest dress I could find—a foreign dress for a foreign girl.

When we got out of the car at church, a group of kids stopped to stare at us.

"Hallo, hallo, hallo," one said to me. How could you answer a greeting like that?

"*A-tok-a*," another yelled. Yes we were pointy noses—foreigners. Did they have to announce it to the whole world?

One little boy came close to A.J. "*A-tok-a*," he said.

"Slanty eyes," A.J. countered, pulling his eyes into narrow slits.

The Chinese kids laughed at that and immediately began making faces. They pulled out their ears, crossed their eyes, stuck out their tongues.

"Enough of that, A.J.," Dad told him. We walked into church.

The Chinese kids hadn't seen enough of A.J.'s tricks. They kept making faces and tempting him to respond. A.J. was obviously trying to figure out some way to entertain his audience without quite disobeying Dad's not-so-specific order. He crossed and rolled his eyes and wiggled his ears. He had the kids almost rolling with laughter—until Dad stopped him again.

A little Chinese girl grinned at me and babbled something in Chinese. I just shrugged and looked away. Sure I felt stupid about not answering, but what could I say?

The little girl walked around to the other side of me, caught my eye, and repeated what she had said.

I pointed to A.J. Let him entertain her. He seemed to be able to communicate with the Chinese. Let him sit with them too. I took Hud and found a seat far in the back.

Sunday school started. I twiddled my thumbs through song after song that I couldn't sing. Hud poked me in the ribs when they started "Jesus Loves Me." I mumbled the words along for Hud's sake. Two weeks earlier I'd been proud to sing the song in Chinese. Now I thought only of my mistakes. The Chinese kids didn't need my help anyway. They almost shouted the song, they knew it so well.

During the lesson I counted floor tiles and tried to think about my peanut butter world where I understood everything.

After Sunday school I followed the other kids outside. Some of the girls started jumping rope out in the street. One girl was spinning round and round, moving the rope in a circle a few inches above the ground. The other girls stood close to her and jumped over the rope as it came close to their feet. The girls laughed as one girl jumped too late and missed. No use in me sticking around. Jump rope was a good way to get your feelings hurt. I went inside and read a book until church started.

I thought the church service would never end. I re-counted the floor tiles until I caught a little girl staring at the hair on my arms. I crossed my arms to hide them and began to make plans to rearrange my bedroom. I really liked my bedroom fine, but it was the only thing I could think of to take my mind off the world around me—a world where I was the only one who didn't fit in.

As soon as Uncle Tim said "Amen" to the final prayer, I got the car keys from Dad and hurried out to the car.

"Two services down, one to go." I sighed and rolled down the window. Minutes later I was soaked in sweat. Didn't my family know it was hot in the car? I bit my lip to keep back the silly tears. I knew I could handle Taiwan if I could just keep my mind on my peanut butter world.

Dinner came and went. I stood up, ready to speed away from the table before Mom got any funny ideas about doing dishes. But Mom stopped me. She excused the rest of the family, but kept me behind.

Didn't she know what a hot job it was doing dishes on a day like this? Right away I knew she did. And it didn't end up being about dishes at all.

"There's something I want to talk to you about," Mom said. "Sit down, please."

I sat, without saying a word. I figured I was in big trouble.

"Amy, I'm puzzled about something. Back in America we always had to watch out for A.J. He's a wonderful entertainer, but he doesn't exactly impress people with his good behavior. I think there's hope for A.J.—well, let's just say he's learning and growing. Anyway, back in America we worried a little about A.J.'s behavior. Hud was shy, and that made for some problems, too. But we never had to worry much about you. You were our first-born, our obedient child who always did everything right."

Mom gathered up the dirty silverware and went on. "But there was more to it than just acting right. You seemed to have a special heart for the Lord, to be eager to serve Him and do what He wanted you to. While A.J. was refusing to come to Taiwan because he'd have to leave Uncle Pete's horse behind, you seemed happy for the chance to be part of our missionary work."

She put the silverware in the sink. "We knew that moving to Taiwan would mean some real changes for you kids. We knew it would take a little time to adjust. We were especially worried, concerned I mean, about Hud and A.J. But you already seemed determined to do your best to adjust and find ways to serve the Lord here."

Visions of Amy Carmichael, disguised as an Indian lady, heroically rescuing little Indian girls, drifted through my mind. My dreams had been good. What had happened to them?

I watched Mom stack the plates. "I've tried to do missionary stuff," I said. "But how can I be a missionary if I don't know Chinese?"

Mom hesitated. "It will take time for you to learn enough Chinese to say much. I know that. But it's your attitude that I'm worried about. Like this morning. You didn't even try to sing the songs during Sunday school. You scowled at every Chinese person who dared to look your direction. And you sat so far away from the Chinese kids in Sunday school, one would have thought they had leprosy or something. What happened?"

I took a quick breath and tried to swallow the tears at the back of my throat. "I want to be friendly," I said. "But how can I when I can't say anything?"

Angry *bu yau*'s filled me with shame. Mom seemed to see right inside of me.

"You don't have to carry on a long conversation with Chinese people," Mom said. "You can't do that—yet. But you can greet them. You can look them in the eye and smile at them. You can't sing a lot of the songs, but you can sing

'Jesus Loves Me.' You can't understand the lesson or sermon, but you don't have to look like it's killing you."

"What about A.J.?" I had to think of something to excuse my actions and give me back a little self-respect. "A.J. calls them 'slanty eyes' and pulls his eyes into slants. Do you call that being friendly?"

"Calling Chinese people 'slanty eyes' is not a nice thing to do." Mom sat down across from me and fiddled with the salt and pepper shakers. "But I don't really think those kids understood what A.J. said. We don't want any of our children to say mean things in any language. And making faces is just another way of communicating. You may not be able to speak Chinese yet, but you can still communicate quite a bit."

"How?"

Mom set the salt and pepper shakers down and stared at the top of my head. I knew she wanted me to look up so she could study my eyes, but it was my turn to play with the salt and pepper shakers. "You may not have said anything to the Chinese people this morning," she said, "but you did communicate. When you frown, act bored, sit away from everyone else, rush to the car after church, you may not be speaking Chinese. But you are communicating very clearly."

"But A.J. . . . ."

"You're not A.J. You never will be, I'm happy to say." Mom smiled. "He's a good boy, deep down, but one A.J. at a time is plenty. However, you do choose what kind of Amy Carmichael Kramer you are going to be. God doesn't expect you to teach Chinese Sunday school or pass out a thousand tracts a month. He expects you to do only what you can—to do well what He puts in front of you. Think about it, will you?"

I nodded. For once I couldn't answer.

I started for my room.

"Amy?"

"Yeah, Mom?"

"I know it's not easy. Making changes never is. Remember, your father and I are making changes too."

I left.

I felt like a failure. All I'd been trying to do was learn how to get along in Taiwan. Jessica had taught me that. Meanwhile I had hurt some people by my unfriendliness. I didn't want to do that again. I needed a plan to put my chop suey world in order. Mom had said I should look people in the eye and smile. If that's what it took to be a good missionary, I'd do it.

I took out a pencil and paper and made a sign:

Successful missionaries

1. Look people in the eye.

2. Smile.

I taped the sign to my wall. That job taken care of, I planned what I would wear to school for the next week.

The sun flooded through my window the next morning and woke me up at 6:03. I checked my clock. Above it flashed my "successful missionary" sign. I promised myself I would not forget today.

Walking to school, I met our neighbor girls in their blue school uniforms, carrying yellow bookbags. They whispered to themselves and stared at us.

I (1) looked them in the eye, (2) smiled, and even (3) said, *"Ni hau?"*

Why did they look so surprised? They had heard me say *"Ni hau?"* before. Of course, my last fifteen or twenty words to them had all been *"Bu yau."* That might explain things. Mom was right. I was coming across as unfriendly, even though I didn't mean to be. I would take care of that.

I tried again. *"Ni hau?"*

"Hau," one of them answered. Was she Mr. Hwang's daughter? I thought I was finally learning to tell the difference between the girls.

When I got to school, Mickey was just going in the gate, and Jessica's van wasn't anywhere in the parking lot. It was a perfect chance. I called to her. "Hi, Mickey."

She turned around and gave me a surprised glance—like the neighbor girls.

"Hi, Amy."

"Did you have a good time in Taipei?"

"Taipei?"

"Yeah. You know. You were going to the zoo and the museum and everything. Did you have a good time?"

"Oh, that. Well, uh, sure. Better than some dumb party."

I should have kept my mouth shut. She obviously hadn't gone to Taipei at all, and I had only reminded her of the party.

How could I cover my mistake? "Uh, sure is hot today."

"Yeah. Let's hurry and see if Mrs. Bronniman is in the room yet."

I turned around to check the parking lot. Jessica's van was just pulling in.

"You go ahead," I told her. After all, I'd already gone beyond looking her in the eye and smiling.

Every time I met someone that day I tried out my two-step formula on them. It really wo,ked. People were actually friendlier than usual. But then it was easy to use the two steps on peanut butter friends. It was my chop suey friends I had to work on.

Mom made sure I got my chance.

When we got home from school that day, the smell of chocolate chip cookies greeted us. Besides baking the cookies, the oven had turned the whole house into one big oven. But it was worth it for our first batch of homemade cookies in Taiwan.

"Mom, I love you. Can I have a cookie?" I asked, reaching for one.

"Not the ones on that plate. Those are for Mr. Hwang," she said.

"Mr. Hwang? Why?"

"Mr. Hwang has been very nice to us. He's given us so many things, I wanted to do something to say 'thank you.' "

I found an approved cookie and bit into it.

"You're trading chocolate chip cookies for cold congee, soybean milk, and a weird hair bow I'm too embarrassed to wear? Of course, there's Hud's tambourine. That's a real contribution to the family." As soon as the words were out of my mouth I wished I could take them back.

"I'm not trading anything. I'm just showing appreciation for his generosity," Mom said. "The things he gave us might not be things that we enjoy much. But Mr. Hwang doesn't know that. He's just trying to be nice. Right now, this is the only way I know of to let the Hwangs know that we care about them. Someday we want to tell them that the Lord loves them. I was hoping you'd take the cookies over to him."

"But I can't say anything."

Mom just gave me a long meaningful look.

"I'll do it for two extra cookies," A.J. bargained.

"I wanted to give Amy the first chance," Mom told him.

"I'll go." I grabbed the plate. I'd goofed a couple of times and given some Chinese the idea I was unfriendly. Here was my chance to make up for it.

I rang the doorbell and Mr. Hwang answered. Immediately he called another man to the door.

"Hello," man number two greeted me. His face was Chinese but his accent was American. "You must be the American girl from next door."

I nodded my head. I was looking him in the eye, but I was too surprised to smile.

"Please come in."

"I, uh, I brought these cookies over for the Hwangs."

"Very good! I'm Mr. Hwang. I guess that means I get to eat them." He took the plate from me.

The man must have seen the confusion on my face. He laughed. "I'm Mr. Hwang's brother," he said. "I live in California. I came back to Taiwan to visit my family. My brother told me he lived next to an American family."

"Oh."

"My brother says he likes living next to Americans. I told him he should talk to you, but he is too embarrassed. He is afraid of making mistakes. He doesn't have many chances to speak English so his spoken English is not good. He can understand a lot, though. You can speak to him in English. Maybe he will try to answer you."

"All right." I looked at Mr. Hwang, our neighbor, and smiled weakly.

Suddenly I remembered something. A.J. and I had made all those rude comments about the congee in front of Mr. Hwang. We thought he didn't know English. He had probably understood every word!

Chapter Thirteen
The Eruption of Mount Jessica

So Mr. Hwang could understand English. I hardly slept that night worrying about what he must think of me after my rudeness yesterday. I tossed and turned and fluffed up my pillow.

I had never meant to hurt him. Of course, if I'd had any idea he understood English, I never would have said those things. Mom and Dad wanted to witness to the Hwangs, and they'd be glad to hear that Mr. Hwang understood some English, but after what I'd said, would he listen?

I'd already found out that here in Taiwan you could insult people without even trying. It must be the difference in culture. Since the Chinese couldn't understand what I said, they listened to my actions instead. I would have to be more careful.

It was too hot to sleep. I threw off my sheet.

I don't want to hurt Chinese people, I thought. I want to be friends with them. But what can I do when I can't speak Chinese?

The answer flashed into my mind. "Mickey's Chinese. You can talk to her."

I really did feel sorry for Mickey. I wished I could say something to make her feel better. How could I be nice to her without making Jessica mad?

Mickey always made things difficult.

Or was Jessica the real problem? Being Jessica's friend had made me popular. She was fun and everyone liked her. But she was bossy. She thought she could tell everyone who to be friends with. It wasn't right.

I pulled the sheet back up because of the air blowing from the fan. If only I could get to sleep! But how could I sleep with an answerless problem on my mind?

I knew one thing. As much as I needed Jessica's friendship, I couldn't let her boss me around anymore. She wanted me to snub Mickey, and I wasn't going to do it. Jessica wouldn't like the idea much, but maybe if I explained it to her she'd understand how I felt.

"Jessica," I'd say. "You're a nice person, but you're just too bossy."

No. That would never do.

I tried it again. "Jessica—you're an excellent friend, my best friend. In fact, you're the best friend I've ever had."

No. That wasn't true. What about Dawn, back in Wyoming? She'd been my friend since church nursery days.

"Jessica, I really appreciate your friendship."

That was true.

"When I came to Taiwan, I worried about making friends more than anything else. But you were my friend from the beginning, and you made the other girls like me too."

Good so far.

"There's just one little problem. You don't seem to like it if I talk to Mickey or even smile at her. I don't want her for my best friend or anything. I don't even care about being good friends with her. After all, she's not my type like you are. But no matter what Mickey is like, I've still got to be friendly to her. That's only right."

What would Jessica think?

I didn't know, but I'd have to take the risk.

I woke up the next morning feeling as if I'd fought with my pillow all night and lost.

"Come on. Get up, Amy," I said to myself. "This is the day you show Jessica you can be nice to Mickey and still be her best friend."

Then I remembered. It was also group project day. Doing a group project with Jessica and Mickey was like working with a pair of smoldering volcanoes.

I fell back onto my pillow. It was a good day to be sick.

All morning long I dreaded geography class, but it came anyway. "We are going to spend our geography time working on our maps," Miss Johnson said. "Let's try to have them done by this weekend, all right?"

I decided that our group would do well to finish at all without a major fight on our hands. We spread our paper out on the table and each of us found a chair closest to what we were drawing.

"Your playground looks good so far," Jessica told Hisako. "You still have a lot left, though. Do you want me to draw the elementary school building?"

Hisako thought a minute. "I might need some help coloring."

"I can help her after I color my buildings," I said.

Jessica looked at Mickey's side of the paper. "You'll probably have to help Mickey. She hasn't even got her rocks drawn yet, and then there's the sign and the front parking lot."

"I can do it in plenty of time if you'll quit being so picky," Mickey said.

"Do it right for a change, and I won't complain," Jessica answered. We started drawing.

Soon Jessica sighed. "Mickey, you're supposed to be drawing rocks, not circles. I told you to make the bottom of the rocks with broken lines. That way it will look like the rocks come out of the ground. Remember?"

"I think they look just fine," Mickey told her. "Your way isn't the only way to draw rocks, you know. You're no artist. You just think you are."

"I know enough about art to know that real rocks aren't circles. Your rocks look like wheels. If they were real, they'd roll right out of the parking lot."

Jessica's anger must have been building up inside her, but I'd been too busy drawing to spot the warning signs.

"I don't know," I said before I realized I was speaking. "I don't think Mickey's rocks are so bad. I kind of like them."

Jessica stopped nagging Mickey to glare at me. She was used to Mickey questioning her viewpoint, but I had never openly doubted her judgment before.

"So *you* don't think I know what I'm talking about either."

What had I gotten myself into?

I started drawing again. "We're never going to get our map done if we spend all of our time arguing. I don't see why you have to make such a big fuss over a couple of rocks. I mean, if you'd do your own stuff and let us do ours, maybe we could get our map done by this weekend."

I glanced up at Jessica. Fury glowed in her eyes. "In other words, 'Mind my own business,' right?"

I shrugged and began to draw again.

"Some friend you are." Jessica slammed her pencil down on the table and stormed out of the room, without even asking permission. Her pencil had scratched a huge mark across the paper; then it clattered to the floor, breaking the uneasy silence.

Every eye watched Miss Johnson to see what she would do. The teacher simply heaved a big sigh. "Class, you only have ten minutes left. See how much you can get done on your maps before the bell rings."

Jessica's outburst had smothered conversations around the work tables, however. Everyone worked in awkward silence until the bell shattered the stillness. It was time for lunch. I wasn't surprised when Mickey asked me to eat with her.

I decided I would. Jessica wouldn't like it much, but then Jessica was already mad. She was going to have to get used to the idea of my being friendly to Mickey. I figured this might be a good way to start things going in a different direction.

Mickey and I went outside to eat lunch by ourselves.

"You sure told Jessica off," Mickey said.

"I didn't really tell her off. I just thought she was getting a little too bossy." I bit into my peanut butter sandwich. "She gets so used to people doing whatever she suggests that she forgets other people might have some good ideas too. Everyone has the right to an opinion."

"That's not what Jessica thinks."

"Sure it is. Jessica's mad right now, but when she cools off and thinks about it she'll realize she wasn't very nice to you."

"You don't know Jessica very well, do you?"

"I like Jessica and I'm glad she's my friend. But I'll have to admit I don't like the way she treats you," I said. "She thinks she can tell me who to be friends with and who I can't be friends with. I don't like that. After she's done being mad and we're friends again, I'm going to tell her that too."

"You *don't* know Jessica very well, do you?" She took a big mouthful of rice and tofu with her chopsticks.

"And another thing," I added hopefully. "I bet I'm not the only one who gets tired of Jessica always telling us what to do. The other girls aren't going to like the way she blew up at me just because I defended you. I wouldn't be surprised if some of them start standing up to her too. Then Jessica can see that people just aren't going to stand for her putting other people down. Maybe it's a good thing this all happened."

"As I said, I don't think you know Jessica very well. Really, Amy, I know it wasn't easy to stand up to Jessica like that. I appreciate it."

She put her hand on my shoulder to comfort me, as if I'd lost my last friend or something. Did she think I was giving up my friendship with Jessica for her? No way. Jessica just needed to learn a few things. After that we'd be the best of friends again.

But the truth was, I really didn't know Jessica all that well.

The bell rang and we went to our next class. Jessica was already seated. She was surrounded by the rest of the sixth-grade girls; they took turns frowning at Mickey and me and hissing to each other in whispers. That was only the beginning. The rest of the school day went the same way. Wherever we went, Jessica and her followers took great pains to ignore us.

I began to worry a little. Jessica didn't seem to be learning her lesson very fast. I'd hoped that by now she'd be admitting her mistakes, apologizing for losing her temper, and asking to start all over again.

But then, what could I expect? She needed time to cool down. Right? Tomorrow maybe we could talk it all over and patch up our differences. After all, what had I done? Simply shown approval for Mickey's rocks and suggested that Jessica work more and complain less. How mad could Jessica be?

The next day came and I found out.

I went to school determined to be friendly and forgiving to Jessica, yet firm in my decision to be friendly to Mickey.

When I got to English class, Jessica was already there. I found an empty seat next to her and sat down.

"That seat is saved for someone," she said.

"Sorry. I didn't know. Who are you saving it for?"

"Anybody but you."

I moved.

In math Mr. Kulp had given us assigned seats. I was seated next to Jessica—until that day. Our seating arrangements had been mysteriously changed.

I wondered how we would ever make it through geography class.

I didn't need to worry. Jessica got a "splitting headache" just in time for class and went to the nurse. The headache lasted exactly an hour. The same thing happened the next day and the rest of the week.

After several days of this I caught Jessica coming out of the restroom by herself and cornered her. "Are you still mad?" I asked.

"You made your choice," she said.

"No. You've got it all wrong. I didn't choose Mickey over you. I still want to be your best friend. I don't even really want Mickey for a friend. I just want to be friendly to her. I don't think it's right to . . . to make her feel like dirt. I just can't be mean like that to anyone. But I still want to be your friend. Really."

While I chattered on, my trembling hands fumbled to braid a lock of hair. Jessica stood silent until my eyes met hers and locked into position. Her eyes held mine, commanding me not to look away. Then she spoke.

"Like I said, you made your choice."

Chapter Fourteen
The Supreme Insult

My chop suey world never had been very terrific, and thanks to Jessica, my peanut butter world was falling apart. I had started the school year as the sixth grade's number two girl, and four weeks later I was in last place. I stumbled through day after day with a horrible empty feeling inside.

After several days of watching me come home grouchy and silent, Mom knew something was wrong. Friday after school she asked me about it.

I told Mom about the group project and Jessica's blowup. "You told me to be kind to Mickey," I said. "Well, I followed your advice. I took Mickey's side against Jessica just once. Now Jessica won't even talk to me. No one else will either."

"Not even Mickey?"

"Sure, Mickey does. But no one else."

I sank into a kitchen chair, pulled off my socks by the toes and dropped them in a forlorn little pile.

Mom sighed. "I'm sorry, Amy. You did the right thing. It's tough now, but don't give up on everyone in the sixth grade. The girls may not be talking to you now— but they will in time."

"You don't know Jessica, Mom."

"No. I guess I don't. I'm not sure I want to. Some of the things you've told me about her make me wonder."

"Funny. I used to think I was so lucky to have Jessica for a friend. Not anymore."

I sighed, and Mom sighed with me. Then she smiled. "Keep your chin up, Amy. Things like this have a way of improving with time. We'll pray that the Lord will work it out. He can even make it into something good."

Pray? Back in Pinedale, I'd prayed for a friend in Taiwan, but I hadn't prayed about this situation at all. I pulled myself out of the chair and started up the stairs for my bedroom. It had become my great escaping place, the place I went to get away from everything and everybody.

"Listen, Amy," Mom called after me. "Why don't I call the Petersons and see if Kelly would like to come spend the night? In all the time we've been here, we've been too busy to have her over. But tonight is free. Shall I call her?"

I didn't answer right away.

Kelly. At first I'd thought she would be my best friend in Taiwan. I thought I would be lonely and need her for a special friend. Then school started and I'd had plenty of friends—for four weeks. Now however, I had to admit that I was pretty desperate.

But even though I needed friends, Kelly didn't. She had lived here all her life. She had Chinese friends and school friends.

We'd both been busy, but I really hadn't tried to get close to Kelly. From the beginning, she had reminded me of an older sister who knew what was best for me. Now, with Jessica and the girls against me, it was getting unbearably lonely. Maybe I should give Kelly another chance.

"I guess you can invite her if you want," I said.

In my room I sat on my bed and wondered how to begin praying. I hadn't really talked to God lately. My prayers had all been the quick kind—empty words with no thought behind them.

"Lord," I whispered. "I'm sorry I've been leaving You out of things. I want to be a good missionary, and while I'm at it, I'd sure like to have some friends too. Please help me to make friends, even if it's just Mickey. And help Mickey to get saved."

Mom invited Kelly and she came. I wondered if Aunt Martha had made her come.

After a supper of fried chicken, we went up to my room and looked for a game to play. Kelly searched through the pile of games and asked what I thought of playing Monopoly. I agreed. We handed out the money and set up the board.

Kelly was just putting her first house on *Boardwalk* when she asked me straight out, "Hey, what's the deal with you and Jessica? I haven't seen you together lately. I thought you were supposed to be best friends or something."

"We were. We got along great until she told me I couldn't have anything to do with Mickey. Jessica didn't even want me to be decent to her. I didn't think that was right. Jessica doesn't have to be Mickey's friend if she doesn't want to. But she doesn't have any right to tell me who to be friends with."

I drew a *Chance* card and went directly to jail, not passing *Go* or collecting two hundred dollars. I spent my jail term explaining about our group project and how Jessica blew up at me.

"Jessica hasn't talked to me since," I said. "She won't let the other girls talk to me either, like she's their boss or something. It works. When Jessica tells them to leave me alone, they don't even look my direction."

"Surprise, surprise." Kelly passed *Go* and took two hundred dollars from the bank.

"What do you mean by that?"

"Jessica has bossed her classmates around from the minute she came to Taichung International in fourth grade. I knew you were in trouble as soon as I saw you running around with her."

"Then why didn't you warn me?"

"What did you want me to do? Tell you not to be her friend? I thought you didn't like people telling you who to be friends with."

Kelly had a point, but that didn't help me now.

"So what am I supposed to do?" I asked her. "I don't speak Chinese, so school is about the only place I really feel comfortable. I used to have lots of friends there, but now Mickey is the only friend I have left."

"Be glad you still have Mickey. If you only have one friend, you'd better be careful what you do with that friend. Your turn, Amy."

I hated to admit it, but Kelly was right. My peanut butter world was the only place I fit in. And Mickey was my only friend in my peanut butter world. If I wanted to fix my peanut butter world, I'd better fix my friendship with Mickey.

Mickey and I weren't much alike, but maybe I could change that. Maybe I could help her see what she was doing wrong and help her fit in around school.

I landed on *Boardwalk*. By now Kelly had built a hotel on it. I counted out two thousand dollars with hardly a thought. Hundreds of pastel-colored dollars might be passing through my hands, but my brain was making plans. Plans to stick my comfortable peanut butter world back together. By the time I'd gone bankrupt and made Kelly rich, my plans were all made. All I had to do then was wait for an opportunity to put my plans into action.

My chance came when Mickey invited me over to her house that weekend. She said that Friday was Moon Festival and she wanted me to spend it with her family. I said I'd be glad to come. I even remembered to slip a tract into my suitcase.

Mickey's house wasn't anything like ours or Jessica's. It was expensive but, I decided, not really pretty. Their living room furniture was huge and padded and expensive-looking, but I didn't like its big, gaudy print.

Mickey and I kicked off our shoes and piled our book bags by the door. Her grandmother brought us some cartons of guava drink and some moon cakes.

"Do you like guava drink?" Mickey asked me.

"What's guava?" I asked, studying the side of the carton.

"It's that fruit there." She pointed to the picture on the carton.

I smelled it. Like so many things here, the juice smelled so different from anything in America that it was impossible to describe the smell, even to myself.

"I don't think Americans eat guavas," I told her.

"What about moon cakes? Do you like them?"

"Is that what you call these little round things?"

"Yes. We always eat moon cakes the week of Moon Festival. Haven't you eaten any yet?"

I shook my head.

"There's pineapple, red bean, egg, lotus seed, and coffee." Mickey ticked off the list of kinds as she sorted through the different packages. "Do you want to try one?"

"Well, um . . . I'm not really hungry right now."

Mickey immediately began chattering away to her grandmother in Chinese. I couldn't understand much of what they said, but I recognized the word for "American" and knew they were talking about me.

"I'll go get us something better to eat," Mickey finally explained to me in English. She obviously didn't believe I wasn't hungry. She picked up the moon cakes and drinks and walked out, leaving her grandmother to shake her head in disbelief at peculiar American tastes. Her grandmother followed her out. I guess she had given up on me.

With Mickey out of the room, I had the chance to study something I'd been too embarrassed to look at. The godshelf.

The godshelf was a tall, narrow table set against one living room wall. An ugly idol about a foot tall stood in the middle of it. On each side of the idol, red light shown dully out of tiny light bulbs. In front of the idol were several incense sticks that had gone out and a little red cup that might have held wine. I didn't know what the other stuff on the shelf was.

When I'd walked around outside at night, I had seen the red glowing lights from godshelves. But this was the first time I had ever been so close to one. It gave me goosebumps.

Mickey came in then and caught me staring at it.

"I found some candy bars and Cokes," she said. "Are you hungry enough for a Snickers?"

"I think I could make room for one," I said. My mouth began to water. I couldn't remember the last time I had eaten a Snickers candy bar. I was going to enjoy this one.

We ate in silence for a few minutes. Suddenly the curtain behind me flapped in the wind. Startled, I jerked around and stared at the godshelf, as if the god had made the noise.

I tried to laugh it off, feeling stupid. "Just the wind. The noise startled me."

Mickey ignored my excuse. "We have the god for my grandmother. My parents only worship to make her feel happy. Grandmother would be very afraid for us to take away the god. Grandmother also says we must worship and respect our ancestors. But it's not a big deal." She shrugged. "I don't care about it."

The thing still gave me a spooky feeling.

"Do you want to go play badminton?" Mickey asked.

"I don't know how to play very well."

"We can just hit it around."

"I don't know."

"How about computer games?"

"I only know how to play the games the school has. Do you have any of those?"

"No." Mickey thought some more. "Do you want to watch TV?"

"There aren't any English shows on now, are there?"

"No."

"Hmmmm."

"So what should we do?"

"I don't know."

"I don't know either."

"I know," I said. "Let's go to your room and fix our hair."

"But we're not going anywhere."

"So? We can just do it for fun."

"But I'm no good at doing hair."

"It's okay. I'll teach you."

Mickey didn't sound too excited about the idea, but there was nothing else to do, so we went to her room.

I brushed through her straight hair, trying to give it some sort–any sort–of style.

"You ought to part your hair on the side and then pull one side back." I tried my new idea. "Or maybe you could brush all of the hair on one side of your head over the top and hold it with a barrette."

I kept brushing her hair and trying it in different styles. There had to be some way to make Mickey look good. Finally she said, "What's wrong with the way I usually wear it? It's easy to fix that way, anyway."

"This way is more stylish. It makes you look older."

"So?"

"Then you should wear that light blue skirt of yours with your blue and white striped blouse."

"But I always wear my gold blouse with that skirt."

"I know. But the striped blouse would look better."

"Why do I have to dress like you want me to?" Mickey said. "Why can't I just dress like I always have?"

"I'm only trying to help. I thought you might want to wear something that's in style, for a change."

I hadn't really meant to say those last three words. But wearing such weird combinations of clothes made it harder for her to make friends. I knew I could help her if she'd just let me. It was time to get on with the rest of my plan. I dug the tract out of my back pocket.

"I brought you something to read."

"What for?"

"Well, I thought you might want to read it. It tells you how to become a Christian."

"What if I don't want to become a Christian?"

No one had ever asked me a question like that. "Well . . . you need to be a Christian, or you won't go to heaven when you die."

"That's what you say." Mickey shrugged. "We Chinese believe that when we die we turn into something else, like an animal or another person or something. If we live a good life now, our next life will be lucky."

Did she really believe that?

"But . . . but that's not true," I cried. "The Bible says when we die our souls either go to heaven, or, well—you know—I can't explain it very well. Would you just read this?" I held the tract closer to her.

"I already know about Jesus," Mickey said calmly. "He was born where they feed animals, with hay and everything. That's Christmas. He died on a cross. That's Easter. Two big American holidays. You Americans have been celebrating Christmas and Easter for a few hundred years. But we Chinese have been worshiping our gods and ancestors for thousands of years. We let you believe what you want to believe. Why don't you let us believe what we want?"

I shook my head. This talk was not going according to plan. "Because it's not true. The Bible says that Jesus is the only way to heaven."

"But our teachers tell us that the Chinese way is true. So how do you know you're right and we're wrong?"

Mickey hadn't taken the tract. I folded it up and put it into my pocket. What could I say when she just wouldn't listen to reason?

"You know, you'd have more friends," I said, "if you wouldn't argue with everything. I'd like to help you, but how can I help if you won't listen to me?"

"You didn't listen to me any more than I listened to you." Mickey looked me right in the eye. "I thought you wanted to be friends. But you'll only be my friend if I do everything the way you want me to. You're just like Jessica!"

Just like Jessica. The words stung—more than a slap in the face. I swung around to hide my burning cheeks. If there was anyone in the whole world I didn't want to be like, it was Jessica Nyquest.

I sank down on the bed and fumbled with my suitcase. My hands trembled as I put my brush inside. I wiped the corner of my eye with my thumb knuckle, hoping Mickey wouldn't notice. Finally she suggested we go outside where her father was starting the hibachi in the front yard.

We barbecued strips of chicken, pork, and squid with Mickey's family. The pork and chicken were good, but I thought the squid tasted like rubber bands. Then we climbed up to the roof and watched the moon, round and white like a giant moon cake. I nibbled the flaky pastry from the outside of the sweet, chewy, weird-tasting moon cakes and thought about what Mickey had said.

Was I really like Jessica?

Mickey's grandmother peeled the thick skin of huge pear-shaped pomelos. Section by section I ate the dry, grapefruit-like fruit. When the time for firecrackers came, I lit my share of them. Although Mickey and I weren't saying much to each other, I stayed up late with her because it was Moon Festival night. Her grandmother said that on this night, the later a girl goes to sleep, the longer her mother will live.

I was spending my first Chinese holiday in Taiwan with a Chinese family, doing all the traditional Chinese things. That should count for something. It didn't sound like something Jessica would ever do.

About midnight we were finally allowed to go to bed. But as tired as I was, questions still crept around the edges of my drowsiness like thieves, robbing my tired brain of sleep.

Much later Mickey's whisper broke through the muffled explosion of firecrackers. "Amy? Are you awake?"

"Yeah."

"If I believe in Jesus will you be my friend? I mean, I will if you really want me to."

"It's not like that," I said. "You can't believe just to be my friend."

"Why not?"

How could I explain it?

I wanted Mickey to be saved. But for her, becoming a Christian was like a bag of M&M's—just another thing to buy friendship.

But what about me? Did I really care about Mickey? Or did I just want her to change so I could have at least one friend in my peanut butter world?

Maybe Mickey was right. As awful as it was, maybe I was just like Jessica.

Chapter Fifteen
Easy, for Once

The next day in my bedroom with my door shut I could finally let out the tears.

"Just like Jessica."

Those three words still hurt. But hard as I tried to argue them away, I knew there was truth in the words. I had only been trying to make friends. There was nothing wrong with that. I had great plans—but they had been my plans, not God's. And the harder I worked on my plans, the more I messed things up. I hadn't even thought about God's opinion of my plans. It was about time I did.

I glanced around my room, wondering where I'd put my Bible. It wasn't on my dresser or on the bookshelves in the section that had devotional books. It wasn't by my bed in the box where I kept the books I was reading. I checked the neat stacks of games in the closet. Everything was labeled, in boxes, and in alphabetical order. But no Bible.

How could I lose my Bible in a room that was organized, alphabetized, and color-coded?

I knelt by my bed and pulled my shoes out of their neat row. Next came the row of boxes wrapped in paper of different colors. As I pulled out the blue box, I saw it. There against the wall was my Bible. I barely remembered it sliding behind my bed one day. But that was . . . how long ago?

Okay, so I had missed having devotions for a few days. Or maybe a little longer. Truth was, once school started, I never had enough time in the morning for devotions.

I picked up my Bible and dusted it with a tissue. It fell open at the bookmark I'd left in the fifth chapter of Mark. I had started the school year reading Mark, a chapter a day. Now I was little behind.

I'll read five chapters to make up for it, I decided.

I read about Jesus healing people and John the Baptist getting his head cut off. That didn't seem to have anything to do with my life in Taiwan in the twentieth century.

Then I came to a part of the story in Mark 6 that I had never noticed before. It talked about Jesus and His disciples going away by themselves in a boat to a quiet place. But many of the people saw where they were going and ran ahead of them to meet them at the next place.

So Jesus got tired of the crowds too. When He tried to escape from them in a boat, they followed Him on foot. He knew what it was like to have people watching His every move.

"But at least Jesus could talk to them," I muttered. "Twenty million people live in Taiwan, and I can't even talk to most of them. After kindergarten and five grades of school, I can't even read and write the language of the place I live in. It makes me feel like a two-year-old all over again."

And then I thought about Jesus. The mighty Son of God created the universe and kept it running for thousands of years. Then He became a man. But not at first. Before He was a man, He was a baby, dependent on His parents. I guessed

that becoming a baby must have made God's Son feel like a foreigner too.

"Thank you, Lord," I prayed. "I guess You do understand. Maybe I just need to be patient and friendly. If I wait a little while, things will work out by themselves and I'll have friends again. Is that right?"

I hoped He was saying yes.

I wasn't done with my five chapters, though. I skimmed through the rest of the chapters and was almost done. Then Mark 10:45 jabbed at my conscience like a giant syringe shooting a dose of medicine into my spiritual veins. And, like the typhoid shot I'd gotten when we came to Taiwan, it hurt.

For even the Son of man came not to be ministered unto, but to minister.

I knew that the word *minister* meant "to serve," and the verse made me uncomfortable, but I wasn't sure why. I was serving God here, wasn't I? I'd been looking Chinese people in the eye and smiling. I'd been friendly to Mickey and even quit trying to change her. What more could I do when I couldn't speak Chinese?

Something was wrong. But no matter how hard I tried, I couldn't figure out what it was.

Now that I had hardly any friends left, school days dragged by. The girls in my class weren't exactly mean to me. They just managed to make me feel unwelcome to join them in anything.

Except for Mickey. She seemed to have forgotten my blundering attempts at changing her and was now my loyal friend. I just wished she wasn't my only one.

Day after boring day went by. But one morning I woke up with the unshakable feeling that this day was going to be different.

A light breeze puffed at our clothes as we walked to school. Fingers of sunlight filtered through the clouds, brightening the day without heating the body. Perfect weather for what might be a perfect day.

When I got to school, Mickey came running up to the gate to meet me. "Amy! Guess what?"

"What?"

"Jessica's going back to the States! She and her mom are flying out on Wednesday. Today's her last day of school."

"That can't be. Her dad was supposed to work here at least through this school year and maybe next."

"Oh, he's staying. But I guess he's going to be traveling a lot, so Jessica and her mom are moving back to Boston."

I couldn't believe it. We hadn't even finished the first quarter of school. Yet already Jessica had become my best friend and my worst enemy, turned all the sixth-grade girls against me, and was now preparing to leave.

"She's really leaving?" I asked Mickey.

"She's really leaving."

"Really?"

"Really."

Yes! Jessica, my number one problem, was flying out of the country on Wednesday. Maybe someday Mickey wouldn't be my only school friend. Was God answering my prayer?

Mickey and I nearly skipped to class.

When we got to the classroom, Jessica was busy telling the other girls about her plans. "Mom says she'll buy me a whole new wardrobe once we get to Boston. We're going to move in with my grandmother. She lives in a beautiful house with a huge yard. Then this summer we're going to stay in my uncle's condo in Florida. We'll get to go to the beach all the time. We'll go to Disney World several times, and Sea World, and Marineland, and Busch Gardens."

Even though Jessica had to change schools in the middle of a school year, it was pretty hard to feel sorry for her.

The rest of the school day all centered on Jessica. Every teacher started class with an explanation of Jessica's leaving our school, as if we didn't already know. Jessica was called to the office several times during class to get records and answer questions. During every break, the sixth-grade girls talked about nothing but Jessica's trip to America.

Jessica came to band class only long enough to explain to the teacher that she'd be leaving.

"Well, I'm sorry you have to leave," Miss Swenson told her. "We'll miss you in the flute section."

It was nice of Miss Swenson to say that, but I didn't believe her. We had lots of flutes. Who needed Jessica? I didn't even look in Jessica's direction as she left the room.

Halfway through band class, Miss Swenson asked me to get some staff paper. Once inside the supply room, I scanned the shelves from top to bottom, trying to find the paper. I didn't find it on the first set of shelves. I was just ready to step around to another row when I heard someone sniffling. Tiptoeing past several rows, I peered around the corner to see who it was. As I reached out to steady myself, a package of clarinet reeds clattered to the floor and Jessica looked up. Blue eye shadow was smeared around her eyes where she'd been rubbing them.

"Uh, sorry," I said. "Miss Swenson sent me to find some staff paper."

Jessica sniffed. "There's not any back here."

"Oh."

Why should I care if Jessica was crying? It wasn't any of my business. Yet a voice inside me whispered that maybe it was my business. "Why are you crying?" I asked.

Jessica's swollen, red eyes flashed. "A lot you care."

"I do care." For some reason I did. "I mean, I'll admit I was kind of mad at you for getting mad at me. Ever since then none of the girls will talk to me. But I don't hate you or anything. Look. Sometimes it helps to talk about your problems."

Jessica just turned away from me. I didn't know what to say. I wondered whether I should just let her have her privacy. But the voice reminded me that Jessica needed a friend even if she didn't deserve one.

"I thought you were excited about going back to America. What's wrong?" I said.

"You think I'm going to tell you and have you blab it to the whole school?"

"I won't tell anyone if you don't want me to."

She turned back to me and searched my eyes for the truth.

"Promise?"

"Promise."

"You'll never tell anyone?"

"Never."

She sighed. "I don't know."

"You can trust me, Jessica," I told her. "You don't have to tell me, but if you do, I won't tell. I promise."

She stared into her lap and tore a damp tissue into shreds. "All right. The real reason we're going back to America is my parents are getting a divorce. Dad is gone all the time, and Mom says she hates living in Taiwan. But I don't really think it's Taiwan that's the problem. When Dad is home, he and Mom fight all the time." She dabbed at her eyes. "I don't know what's wrong. Maybe they don't love each other any more."

Jessica began to cry all over again. I knelt down beside her and awkwardly laid one hand on her shoulder.

"I'm so sorry," I said. And I was. I couldn't imagine how awful it would be to have your parents get a divorce. All this time I'd been thinking how lucky Jessica was. Not anymore. "I can see why you feel—I mean—if my parents, well, I'd just. . . . Don't worry. I won't tell. I just hope when you get to America. . . . Well, I sure am sorry."

"I'm sorry, too," Jessica said. "About, you know, being mad and everything."

"It's okay. It's over with now."

Then I checked my watch and realized I'd been gone from class for quite a while. Miss Swenson would be expecting me back by now. I wanted to help Jessica, but I couldn't think of anything else to do.

"I'd better get back to class, or Miss Swenson will come looking for me," I said. "But I hope things go better for you in America."

Quickly I searched the shelves, found the staff paper, and jogged back to class.

Band was our last period of the day. I left school right after band, and I never saw Jessica again.

For a few days, class seemed empty without her. The sixth-grade girls were used to waiting to see what Jessica would do and following her. Now they had to make their own decisions. It wasn't long, however, before the girls quit talking about Jessica. It was as if she had never been in our class. It amazed me how someone who was so much the center of the class could be forgotten so quickly.

One day when Mickey was absent, I tried sitting with the other girls for lunch. They didn't seem to mind. Hisako even said she liked my T-shirt.

In P. E., Grace picked me to be on her soccer team right after she picked Susan and before three other girls had been chosen.

Then the next time we had a choice of art projects, I spoke up right away. I wanted to do paper cuttings this time. The other girls decided that they would too.

I was starting to have friends again. At this rate, before long I'd be able to choose a best friend again, instead of taking the only one who would have me. It felt good to be a part of things again—until I remembered why Jessica had left. I couldn't feel good about that.

Still, I had done what I could for Jessica. Now she was gone and so were my problems. All this time I had been worrying about my peanut butter friends for nothing. It looked like God had taken care of the situation for me. My peanut butter world was back together again.

And my chop suey world? I couldn't avoid it all together. But I had that figured out too. All I had to do was look people in the eye and smile. And be careful not to do anything to hurt anyone. I could do that much.

After nearly two months in Taiwan, I knew where I fit in. Now that I had solved that problem, I could be a good missionary and enjoy living in Taiwan at the same time.

I was sure of that.

Absolutely.

Not a doubt in my mind.

Until Black Thursday.

Chapter Sixteen
Black Thursday

Black Thursday is not a Chinese holiday. It's just a name I gave to the worst day in my entire life.

When I woke up on Black Thursday, rain was pounding on our roof. That meant a day of frizzled hair and dodging puddles. Nothing really terrible happened at school, but nothing good happened either. Everyone was in an awful mood. By the time three o'clock came, the sky had cleared up some, but people's moods hadn't.

"Did you have a nice day at school?" Mom asked when I got home. I pushed my way past my brothers' wet shoes and book bags which were blocking the doorway.

"I've had better. What's to eat?"

"There are some cookies in the cupboard. I found a new kind at the store that looked pretty good. I thought we'd give them a try."

While I inspected the cookies, Mom called from the living room. "Oh, I almost forgot. You got a letter from Dawn. I taped it to the refrigerator."

I dropped the package of cookies on the table and leaped over to the refrigerator. Finally—a letter from Dawn! I had written her describing what happened with Mr. Hwang after my last attempt to play Chinese jump rope. I had tried to explain to her what Taiwan was like. It wasn't as cheery as my first letter, but it was honest. That was about a month ago. I had begun to wonder if she'd ever write me back.

I ripped the envelope open, yanked out the letter, and read it as fast as I could.

But the more I read, the more disappointed I became. I had thought my best friend, or rather my former best friend, would be more understanding. I had written to her about my problems and she had answered with this insulting letter. Could I have read it wrong?

I read it again, this time more slowly, looking for things that I could have misunderstood. It still sounded as if my best friend had turned on me.

I didn't know what to think. I looked up to see Hud and A.J. stuffing their faces with cookies, singing with their mouths full. I had to get out of there.

I headed for the door, putting the letter into my pocket. "I'm going for a walk."

Mom didn't look up from the paper she was reading. "Okay."

I was just closing the gate when she stuck her head out the door. "Amy, wait. Where are you going? I don't want you to get lost, you know."

"Don't worry," I told her. "I'll just go down past the big temple and that rice field. Then I'll circle around and come home. I know my way."

"Okay. Just be sure to watch where you're going."

As if Mom needed to remind me. Getting lost in the market that time had been enough for me. Now I didn't go anywhere by myself unless I knew the way as well as I'd known my way around Uncle Pete's ranch back in Pinedale.

I shuffled down a block and a half and turned at the *poki* store. Besides Chinese popsicles, it had toilet paper, cookies, crackers, and candy. That was about all—unless you counted weird Chinese food like congee and dried sour balls and watermelon seeds. That stuff was so different from what I was used to.

Different. The same word I had just read in Dawn's letter. "I thought you were excited about going to live in another country," she'd written, "because you'd see how different people live, and learn to speak a different language, and eat new kinds of foods. Now you don't seem to like Taiwan because it's so different. I don't understand."

When I'd written my letter, I didn't like Taiwan. Now I was learning to like it better. Why? Because I'd ignored the different things in Taiwan and made a little American world of my own where I could be comfortable. But Dawn's letter hinted that I was supposed to like Taiwan because it was so different. Well, she was right about one thing. She didn't understand. "Different" sounds exciting until you have to live with it every day.

I passed the big temple with its red pillars and golden tile roof that sloped into curves at each corner. Normally I loved the beauty of these Chinese-style buildings, even though I didn't go along with the worship that went on inside. But today the temple was another reminder of how different Taiwan was. It helped me know when to turn, and that's all I cared about.

Dawn's letter still spoke to me. "Sounds to me like people have been pretty nice to you. I can't believe all the things they've given you. Of course, you're not going to like every-thing they give you. Of course, their food is going to taste different."

Did she expect me to be thankful for all the weird stuff Chinese people had given me? "Don't preach at me, Dawn McGill," I mumbled. "You don't know what 'different' is until you've eaten cold congee and squid and black jello."

I hadn't really eaten black jello, but I'd heard about it. It was made out of some kind of "fairy grass" that grew in the mountains. It was supposed to make you feel cooler in the summer. Even Kelly hated black jello, and she'd lived here all her life.

I angled down the road by the rice field. I liked rice fields. They were so pretty and green and natural, like gigantic lawns that never got mowed. Uncle Tim said that there used to be a lot of rice fields in this area, but now it was almost solid houses and apartments one right after another. Maybe I'd like Taiwan better if there were more rice fields near us.

After the rice field came streets so crowded with cars and cycles that I could hardly get by. "Why can't they build sidewalks in this country?" I whispered. No one was around to hear me anyway. "And when they do build them, why does everyone have to park all over them? You can hardly walk down the street. I didn't have any trouble walking down the street in Wyoming."

From the back of my mind came some information I'd read in an encyclopedia before we came to Taiwan. I'd been comparing Wyoming to Taiwan to see what my new home would be like. Wyoming had four people per square mile and

Taiwan had over a thousand. Funny, at the time I had thought that was pretty neat. Now I knew it just meant there wasn't much space for anything you could get along without.

Then I saw something really strange. I couldn't figure out what it was at first. Some people were in their front yard cutting up something. They seemed to be butchering an animal. I stared. I'd seen people cutting up animals in the market, but never in the front yard. What kind of animal was it anyway? A pig? No. Maybe a goat? No. It was—

I remembered something Kelly had said. "At the beginning of winter, some Chinese people eat dogs. They think the meat will keep them warm."

A dog! These people were butchering a dog so that they could cat it!

I clapped one hand over my mouth and ran to the other side of the street. How could anyone do that? To eat dog meat was bad enough, but to butcher a dog in your own front yard. . . . How could they?

I sped past the dragon eye tree.

I felt like throwing up, but I managed to notice that I was passing the house where they raised chickens. That was important, because after one more block I needed to turn. A rooster squawked a greeting from his cage as I passed.

By now I was breathing hard. I slowed down and tried to think about something, anything, except dogs and Chinese butchers.

At the end of the block it didn't look like the right place to turn yet. Oh well, it must be another block. I walked past that block and it still didn't seem right. I was beginning to get scared when I saw the big road ahead.

I smiled a little. I knew the way home from the big road. I would just walk down to the motorcycle shop and turn towards the factory with those noisy metal presses. That would get me back on the road I had planned to use.

I decided to be more careful this time, though. Seeing that dog butchered had made me stop thinking for a few minutes, and I could have gotten lost. I shuddered to think about it.

I found the motorcycle shop on the big road. A greasy mechanic was out front taking a tire off a motorcycle. The shop looked a little different from the last time I had noticed it, but I figured that was because he was working on different motorcycles than before.

At the shop I checked both directions to see which way it was to the factory with the metal presses. I tried one way for about a block, and that didn't work, so I tried the other direction. After a few blocks I heard the loud *ka-chink, ka-chink* of metal presses. I frowned. The little factory seemed to be making a different kind of metal things now.

From the factory I looked down the road to make sure the noodle seller's cart was parked where I expected it to be. I saw it, or thought I did, but when I got there, stinky tofu was sizzling in hot oil. Its sour smell reached up to my nose as if to convince me that this really was not the noodle stand.

I stopped then and turned in every direction, considering each way to see if it could be the way home.

"Don't panic," I told myself. "Just think." I grabbed a lock of hair and twirled it round and round my finger, trying to figure out what had gone wrong.

Was the factory I had seen the one that was near our house? The motorcycle shop looked like any other motorcycle shop.

Could it have been a different one? Now I wasn't even sure if the big road was the same big road that was near our house.

I remembered passing the house with the chickens in front, but I had only looked at the chickens, not at the house. And there must be many dragon eye trees in the area.

How could I be sure of anything when the streets looked so much alike? I bit my knuckle to keep from crying. Then I noticed that the man selling the stinky tofu was staring at me. I couldn't explain to him why I was just standing there, and I couldn't ask him for help. I also didn't like having him stare at me.

"I'd better backtrack and find out where I went wrong," I told myself.

Slowly I walked back to the big road and looked both directions. I turned down the big road the way I had come. Soon I saw a little roadside temple that looked kind of familiar. At the temple I spied a familiar looking dog. Then a fruit stand and a truck and a barber shop. Each new thing looked like something near my house.

At last I came to a bakery, and then I realized two things: (1) The bakery was green and red, not pink and white, which meant it was the wrong bakery. I had never seen this bakery before. That meant that the temple, dog, fruit stand, truck, and barber shop were also wrong. And, (2) I was now not only lost, but I had learned that trying to backtrack was a bad idea for anyone who got lost as easily as I did. I'd better stand still while I was still in Taichung, or my parents would never find me.

"Don't panic," I told myself. "There's always something to do." I reviewed what my kindergarten teacher had told us to do if we ever got lost.

"Find a policeman," she'd said. What was her name—Miss Nugent? Six years ago I had thought I'd never forget her name.

"If you can't find a policeman, knock on the door of the nearest house," she'd told us.

"Sorry, Miss Nugent," I whispered. "They don't knock much here. And even if they did, no one would understand a word I said."

"The Chinese are very helpful." It was Aunt Martha's voice I heard echoing through my mind this time. "If you ever need help just ask someone, and if they can't speak English, they can probably find someone who does."

"That's great, Aunt Martha," I told the smiling figure in my mind. "But even if I found someone who could speak English, how would that help? I don't know where I live. I don't even know my address. The Chinese street names are too hard to memorize." (Right then I promised myself that, hard or not, I'd try to memorize them if I ever got back from being lost.)

Then I remembered. I had forgotten to pray—again. So I did. Nothing fancy, you know, but I didn't think the Lord liked fancy prayers anyway.

I leaned against someone's front gate to wait for His answer. I might as well be comfortable while I waited, I thought. I even hummed a little tune.

I don't know what I expected to happen. If a road map had fallen out of the sky, I wouldn't have been able to find my way home. As it was, not even that happened. After about fifteen minutes I began to get cold. I walked around a little and searched for someone who might know me. I would have given anything, just then, to see one of my chop suey friends. Any one of them could have gotten me home.

Finally I did run into someone I had seen before. It was the man selling stinky tofu. If only he could help. But he had no idea where I lived. He didn't sell anywhere near our house.

He grinned at me, showing off teeth stained red by years of chewing betel nut, a kind of Chinese chewing tobacco.

That didn't help.

My feet hurt. I was tired. And hungry. Then the wind came up, making me shiver.

When I tried to find a sunny spot, I noticed that it was getting darker. Lately it had been quite dark by 6:15 in the evening. Chinese kids had to ride their bikes home in the dark from cram school where they went for extra classes. I looked at my watch. 5:58.

Though I tried to stop my tears, a couple of them trickled down my face. Footsteps slapped against the pavement and wheels squeaked. I glanced up to see how God had answered my prayer.

It was the stinky tofu man. He smiled broadly and held out a piece of stinky tofu. His gesture told me he wanted me to take it—free.

I tried to smile as I took it from him. "I don't mean to be picky, Lord," I prayed. "But this isn't really what I had in mind."

Chapter Seventeen
Good-by Chop Suey

The sky got darker as I wandered around shivering, watching for anything that was the least bit familiar. Failing to find that, I began to wonder what to do with the stinky tofu the man had given me. I wasn't too fond of regular tofu, so I imagined stinky tofu would be particularly disgusting. I didn't have any place to throw it, however, and I had no idea when I'd get my next meal. So I decided I'd better save it just in case I got really desperate.

I glanced at my watch again. 6:13. Not that it did me any good to know that. I should have left my watch at home and brought a compass instead.

I searched the street for a place to sit and ended up on a planter that had scratchy tree branches. Finally, for lack of anything else to do, I took a bite of the stinky tofu.

Actually, it wasn't too bad. Not nearly as bad as it smelled.

6:28 had flashed on my watch when I heard someone yelling, *"A-tok-a!"*

I glanced up to see Mr. Hwang's daughter and a friend riding their bikes. They slowed and stopped. I could imagine them wondering why this strange "pointy nose" was sitting on a planter in the middle of nowhere.

The neighbor girl would know her way home! I just had to figure out how to say, "I'm lost. Will you help me?" Only I didn't know how to say "lost" or "help."

I counted off all the Chinese words I knew on my fingers: *Hello, goodbye, thank you, I want, I don't want, I know, I don't know.*

Yes! I could say, "I don't know." That was, *"Wo bu jr dau."* And *"dzai na-li"* meant "where"—or "there" depending on which tone you used. Now which one was correct? I decided I'd better try either one before they left.

Pebbles scattered across the pavement, stirring me from my language review. I looked up to see their bikes disappearing around a corner. I chased after them, but by the time I got to the corner they were way ahead of me. I wanted to yell to them, but I didn't know what to say. I didn't even know the neighbor girl's name. We had always called her "neighbor girl" among ourselves, and I had never bothered with her name when I talked to her.

Soon they were gone. My only hope had ridden away before I had figured out how to say I was lost!

I shuffled back to the planter and plopped down once more. Somehow it seemed darker and colder and more hopeless than before.

"I guess I deserved that, Lord," I prayed. Tears were streaking down my face, but I didn't care anymore. I'd given up trying to be brave. "I know I haven't been very nice to the neighbor girl. I refused to play with her even when she came to my house to ask me. I've lived next to her for almost two months and I still don't know her name. I've been so busy making peanut butter friends that I have quit caring about trying to be friends with her. It's not easy to make a friend in Chinese, but please, Lord, if you'll just help me find my way—"

Screeching brakes interrupted my prayer.

"A-tok-a!"

The neighbor girl! That excellent, sweet, kind, knows-her-way-home neighbor girl. She must have come back just to make sure I was okay, and stopped when she saw me crying. Now what was it I had planned to say?

"Uh, *so bu jr dau,* uh *dzai na-li,*" I said.

She started at me in confusion. *"Dzai na-li? Shem-ma dzai na-li?"*

I wanted to know "where." She wanted to know "where was what?"

"Wo," I answered pointing to myself. I didn't know where I was. Could she understand that? Then I remembered that Chinese pointed to their noses to say "me" and I was pointing to my chest like any American would.

"Wo." I repeated pointing to my nose. *"Wo bu jr dau wo dzai na-li."*

I'm sure I said it all wrong, but she put two and two together and motioned for me to get on the back of her bicycle.

The neighbor girl bumped and wobbled over one street after another. About fifteen minutes later, I found myself in front of my very own home.

"Sye-sye ni," I told her as she came to a stop and I hopped off the back of her bike. How could I tell her how thankful I was? *"Sye-sye ni,"* I said again to her while I prayed silently, "And thank you, Lord, for sending her."

She shrugged, parked her bike, and went into her house.

Mom burst out of the house. "Amy!" she cried, "Are you all right? Where have you been? We've been so worried!"

"I'm okay," I said. Dad opened the door then, and A.J. and Hud were looking out too.

"You should never—"

"Please, Mom, don't scold." I dabbed at the new tears that were threatening to spill over. "I tried to be careful, but I got lost anyway. Our neighbor girl helped me. What's for supper? All I had was a piece of stinky tofu."

I noticed some neighbors peering out their windows. When Mr. Hwang came out to gaze curiously at us, Mom decided we should go in.

The familiar aroma of spaghetti greeted me at the door and promised me I wouldn't be hungry for long. We prayed, thanking God for the neighbor girl and my rescue, Then I ate. Well, I tried to eat, but lifting the fork to my mouth seemed to take more energy than I had. After one helping of everything, I excused myself and went to my room.

I lay across my bed, pulled Dawn's crumpled letter out of my pocket, and read it again. My eyes stopped when I got to the last line. "Anyway, I thought you said missionaries are supposed to win souls, not have fun."

It seemed like years and years had passed since I'd said that to Dawn. The mission field had certainly turned out to be a lot different than I'd expected. When I came, I'd thought it would be no fun at all. But here I was, two months later, expecting it to be nothing but fun.

For even the Son of man came not to be ministered unto, but to minister.

Now I knew what bothered me about that verse. It mean that I wasn't in Taiwan just to make a comfortable life fo myself. There were many good things about living in Taiwan but I wasn't here just to have fun. God had a job for me tc do wherever He placed me. Of course. How could I have missed it?

"Different." "Win souls." "Have fun." The words spur round and round in my mind. I had been angry when I firs read Dawn's letter. Now I knew that I was lucky to have a friend like her. I decided to sit down and answer her lette right away.

Dear Dawn,

I learned three things today.

1. If you don't know your address by heart, don't leave home without it in your pocket.

2. Chinese people can be pretty nice when you give them a chance. And,

3. Stinky tofu would taste okay if you could plug your nose when you ate it.

I also got your letter, which reminded me that I've got some other stuff to learn too. Like when I told you "Missionaries are supposed to win souls, not have fun." I admit I haven't had much fun since I came to Taiwan, but maybe that's because I've been afraid of anything that's different. I've been trying to live my life like I'm still in America and I think that made me miss out on a lot. Different can be okay too.

I've been trying to figure out how to be a good missionary. For a while I thought that if you couldn't speak Chinese, it meant just looking people in the eye and smiling. Now I know that smiling at the Chinese doesn't do much good if you don't like them. Maybe I'll forget about being a good missionary and try to be a good Christian.

Before I came to Taiwan I heard missionaries talk about having a "burden for souls." It sounded so spiritual. But now I know that it means caring about people and wanting them to be saved. Souls are just ordinary people. Like Mickey.

Mickey isn't interested in getting saved—she just wants me to be her friend. I figure if we become good friends, maybe someday she'll become a Christian too. But getting her saved isn't the only reason I want to be her friend. When I think about it, she's been pretty nice to me in her own funny way. No matter how I treated her, she still wanted to be my friend. And I don't even have to wait until I can speak Chinese to talk to her. . . .

I couldn't think of anything else to say to Dawn. I kept thinking about Mickey. She had tried so hard to be my friend. In return, I'd been just-like-Jessica, and I'd treated her like the great American lowering herself to speak to a poor little piece of chop suey. I'd never apologized for the way I acted at her house. After that I'd treated her better, but I was still ready to dump her once I made new friends.

Funny thing was, my other school friends had been peanut butter friends. But even though Mickey spoke English and loved M&M's, she had just been more chop suey. It was amazing she hadn't lost interest in my friendship long ago.

What could I do to make things right with Mickey? I didn't know where to begin. Or did I?

The Bible explained how to make things right with people. It wasn't exactly easy. And I couldn't really do it properly with Mickey if I treated her like I was better than she was.

I put the letter to Dawn away and lay across my bed, thinking.

"Lord," I whispered, "thank You for all the things You've been showing me. Teach me how to really care about people—and how to be a good friend to Mickey. What should I say to make it right with her?"

The next thing I knew, it was morning. A tiny ray of sunshine shone in my window, waking me up and sending hope of a day when the clouds wouldn't rule the sky.

I traded yesterday's clothes, which I had fallen asleep in, for my favorite Wyoming T-shirt, the one with the antelope on it. "Yesterday was terrible," I told myself, "but I'm not about to let today be a repeat of Black Thursday."

All day long I looked for a chance to talk to Mickey alone, but we were always surrounded by people. I decided I'd have to make my own time. During art, when the others were putting their paper cuttings away, I kept cutting on my tiger. That way I'd be the last one out of class. As always, Mickey waited for me.

"Your tiger looks really good," she told me as we started for our next class. "I knew paper cuttings would be better than making stupid clay pots. I'm glad Mr. Wu gave us another chance to do them. Now that Jessica's not here to tell everybody what to do, we can do what we want to do."

"Jessica made some mistakes," I said. "We all do. But now that she's gone, let's forget about it, okay?"

"Well, okay. But I'm still glad she left. Aren't you?"

I didn't hate Jessica anymore, but I was glad she was gone. I didn't want to admit it, though. "I don't know. I feel kind of sorry for Jessica," I said.

"Sorry for Jessica? You've got to be kidding."

"Everyone thinks Jessica's so lucky. But she's never lived in one country for more than a few years. Every time she moves, she loses all her friends. After this she won't get to see her dad very often. She doesn't have any brothers or sisters. She must be kind of lonely."

Mickey kicked a weed that dared to stick its head over the edge of the walkway. "You worry about Jessica if you want, but I'm not going to. Before long all the sixth-grade girls in Boston will be following her around, asking her what to do."

"Maybe. People do follow her. But that doesn't mean they like her. Jessica acts tough, but I don't know. Sometimes I wonder if she acts bossy as a cover-up. Maybe deep down she's really scared."

"Jessica Nyquest? Scared?"

"Yeah. Even Jessica. Changing countries all the time isn't easy. I know. This year, living in Taiwan has been a big change for me. You can't imagine how different it is from Wyoming. And not being able to talk to people and everything—it's kind of scary."

I spotted the coppery shine of a one NT coin that someone had dropped, and I squatted down to pick it up. When we first came to Taiwan, I would have called the coin a penny because it looked a lot like one. But Chiang Kai-Shek's head didn't look anything like Abraham Lincoln's, now that I'd been here a couple of months. I gave the coin a flip, caught it, and stuck it in my pocket.

"My brother A.J. does okay," I went on. "He's always been brave. If he doesn't know the right Chinese word to say, he gets his message across somehow. But me, I'm different. Sometimes I get scared. And when you're scared or hurt, it's easy to hurt other people."

"But that's not right!" Mickey pounded a fist into an open hand. "Even if Jessica is scared, that doesn't give her the right to hurt other people."

"I know. It's not right. Just easy. I've been doing the same thing—worrying about myself so much that I forgot about everyone else. In fact, I want to apologize to you, Mickey."

I started a braid in my hair. My stomach began to flip-flop, but I told it that missionaries had to be brave. Even ordinary Christians had to do scary things. This was one of them.

"I don't really know how to say this," I went on. "But, uh, I haven't been acting like a very good friend to you. I mean, you've been a friend, but, well, you see I had peanut butter friends and chop suey friends. And I never treated my chop suey friends nearly as well as my peanut butter friends. You know what I mean?"

Mickey stared at me. "No. Are you talking about friends or sandwiches?"

"Friends. You see I've been calling my American friends my peanut butter friends because it's easy to be friends with them. I'm used to them—like peanut butter. They are like me. They think like I think and talk like I do. So you can guess who my chop suey friends are."

"No. What's chop suey?" she asked.

I stopped fiddling with my hair. "You're Chinese and you don't know what chop suey is?"

"No."

"But in America, chop suey and chow mein are the most famous Chinese dishes. You can get them at any Chinese restaurant."

"That's American Chinese, not real Chinese."

"Really?"

"Yeah."

I laughed. "I can't believe it. My chop suey friends don't even eat chop suey!"

Either Mickey didn't get the joke, or she didn't think it was funny. She just stood there, waiting for me to go on. Oh, well. I'd made it through my apology and Mickey still wanted me for a friend.

Which reminded me. "Hey, can you come over Friday night?" I said. "Mom says we can bake cookies if we want "

"Chocolate chip?"

"Maybe. I'll ask her."

"Good. My mother can't even bake. Chinese women never bake. They just buy stuff at the bakery."

"I need your help too," I said. "We have this neighbor girl. I want to be her friend but I don't even know her name. She's been real nice to me, but I—well— I kind of need to apologize for something, and I want to make sure she understands. Would you help me talk to her since you know Chinese?"

"That's easy. Is that all you want?"

I thought for a minute. Helping me talk to the neighbor girl was only a beginning. There was a lot that I wanted to learn and do. "That's all for now," I said. "But since we're friends, we can do lots of things together. Okay?"

"Okay. As long as I don't have to eat peanut butter all the time."

I laughed. Sure, my peanut butter friends would never be the same as my Chinese friends. But I had a wide variety of peanut butter friends, and I was beginning to realize that my Chinese friends weren't all alike either. Friends came in all kinds of flavors. And all of them were good.

Games

Chinese children play many different games with a rubber band jump rope like Amy had. Here's how you can make a rope of your own.

Start with at least sixty rubber bands of the same size, about one-and-a-half or two inches in diameter. If you are going to use the jump rope for games in which more than one person jumps at a time, you will need to use more rubber bands. To make a chain using these rubber bands, Chinese kids usually double them, using two bands for each link, but you can also use one for each link or use thick rubber bands rather than thin ones. A rubber band in the normal position forms the first link. To form the second link, put one end of another rubber band through the first one. Bring the two looped ends of the second rubber band together. Then put a third rubber band through the link formed by the second rubber band, and so on. Keep adding links until the chain is eight to ten feet long.

To keep the chain from falling apart, you must knot the last link. When you have the two ends together on the last link, bring one end through the loop of the other end and pull until it is tight.

Now you are ready to play. Chinese children play a wide variety of games with a rubber band rope. Many of these games don't really have rules or winners and losers. They are just things children do with the rope. Rules and ways of playing may vary from one neighborhood to the next. Following are some games Mrs. Brammer has seen Chinese children play.

Chinese Jump Rope

This is the game Amy played: Tie the ends of the jump rope so that it forms a loop. Then have two players stand opposite each other with the rope around their ankles. The rope should be taut, but not stretched tighter than normal.

A third person jumps. When you jump, call out the name of the steps as you jump. These are the names of the jumps in their order: *2, 4, 6, 8, In, Out, On, Out, Twist, Untwist,* and *Done.*

2 and *6:* Jump with both legs at the same time so that you land with your right foot inside the loop and your left foot to the left of the loop.

4 and *8:* Jump the same way, only land with your left foot inside the loop and your right foot to the right of the loop.

In: Land with both feet inside the loop.

Out: Land with a foot on either side of the loop.

On: Land with one foot on each length of rope. This is easiest if you land on the rope with the middle of your foot and keep your toes pointed out.

Twist: With one foot on either side of the rope and facing forward, jump around so that you are facing the opposite direction with your ankles catching the rope.

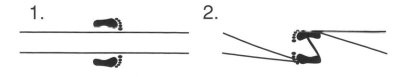

Untwist: Reverse the above move.

Done: Jump over the rope to one side.

If you do all of these steps without missing, have the players holding the rope move it to their knees and try again. Then you can try it again with them holding it around their waists. When you miss, you must hold the rope while one of the other players takes a turn jumping.

High Jump

Have two players hold the rope in their hands so that it makes a straight line above the ground, ankle high. The other players should take turns jumping over the rope. When each has jumped once, the rope is raised halfway between ankle and knee level. After each has jumped, it is raised again to the knees, then to the mid-thigh, then to the waist, and so forth, until a player misses by touching the rope as he jumps or by failing to jump over the rope. When a person misses, he is out of the game. When only one player can jump over the rope at a certain level without missing, he is the winner.

Limbo

This is the same game as high jump, only in reverse. Two people hold the rope parallel to the ground, shoulder high. Each player walks under the rope by walking forward and bending his head backward. If he touches the ground with any part of his body except his foot or if he touches the rope, he is out. After each player has gone through once, the rope is lowered—first to the elbow, then to the waist, and so forth. When only one player can walk under the rope at a certain level without missing, he is the winner.

Cartwheel Jump

Two players hold the rope ankle high while other players reach across the rope and do cartwheels over it. The rope is then raised to the knees, waist, elbow, shoulder, and so forth. A player may touch the rope with the middle of his body, but his hands and feet must not touch the rope, and he must get over in one try. If he misses, he is out. The last one to do a cartwheel without touching the rope is the winner.

Group Jump Rope

Many players may jump at once in this game. One player swings the rope by holding one end of the rope in one hand and spinning around so that the rope makes a circle around him. He should bend over so that most of the rope sweeps across the ground as he does this. The other players stand near the player who is turning the rope, and they jump over the rope as it comes to their legs. If the rope touches a player's legs, he is out. When only one person is left, he is the winner.

Skipping Rope

You may play this kind of jump rope the same way you play it in America. Have two players hold the opposite ends of the rope and swing the rope around while the third jumps over the rope every time it hits the ground. Or you may hold both ends and swing it yourself while you jump. One way Chinese children do it with only two people is a combination of these two. Have a friend swing one end while you take the other. Both swing the rope while one jumps over it at the same time. If you are jumping, you will want your friend to stand on the side of you that is not holding the rope.

Push of War

Chinese children play many games using the jump rope to tie themselves together at the wrists, ankles, and so forth.

This is one of them. It is the opposite of tug of war. Have two players face each other and put the palms of their hands together. Tie their hands together at the wrists. They should each get a good solid stance with their feet apart. At the word "go," they try to push each other over. If either moves his foot, he loses.

Choosing Who Goes First

When you begin a game, you have to decide who goes first. Or you might need to choose a person for some other reason. This is how Chinese children choose:

If they have more than two people playing, they first narrow it down to two by playing a color game. Decide on two colors, like blue and green. Each person pats his chest while saying, "Blue, green, blue."

The second time *blue* is said, each person puts out his hand with his palm either up or down. Everyone who holds out his hand palm up is a "green." Everyone who holds out his hand palm down is a "blue." Whichever color is chosen by fewer players is the loser and those players drop out. Those left choose again, chanting, "Blue, green, blue." This is continued until only two people are left.

The two that are left play *jong-kong-pai* like Kelly and A.J. did. *Jong-kong-pai* seems to be the name given by Americans living in Taiwan although no one knows why. The Chinese, however, call the game *tsai-chywan* or more often "scissors, rock, paper."

If you have never played it before, this is how it goes: Two people shake their fists on an even beat once, twice, then make a scissors, rock, or paper motion. (To make a pair of scissors, form a *v* with your first two fingers. A fist is a rock. A hand held out flat is paper.) American kids in Taiwan sometimes say *jong* on the first beat, *kong* on the second, and *pai* on the third. Chinese say, "scissors, rock, paper." You may say "one, two, three," or you can simply do the motions.

Who wins? "Rock breaks scissors, scissors cut paper, paper covers rock."

Tiger Paper-Cutting Instructions

1. On the following pages are two tiger designs, one more difficult than the other. Enlarge the picture you have chosen. If you use a photocopier, enlarge the design 200%. Your tiger picture will be about 14" high and will fill up a piece of ledger-sized paper.

2. Use a pair of sharp scissors with very thin blades, a razor blade, or an X-Acto knife to cut away the white parts of the design. Be sure to make the cuts that are inside the design first. Then cut along the outline of the design. Leave the black part in one piece. If you wish, use a black marker to blacken the cut edges of your design. (NOTE: If you use anything besides scissors, be sure to place your picture on a piece of heavy cardboard before you begin to cut.)

3. When you have cut out all of the white parts, glue pieces of colored paper behind your design. The colors you will need depend on which design you chose. For example, use pieces of green paper for the bamboo leaves and the eyes of the tiger. Then use white pieces for the eyebrows, ears, clouds, chin, and side sections of the tiger's face. Use a yellow piece of paper to fit behind the moon and a large piece of orange paper for the tiger's face and body. Make sure your colored pieces completely cover the specific section but do not protrude into other sections.

4. You may choose to glue your completed design onto a large piece of white or colored background paper. Then your tiger is ready to display.